S0-BOE-388

Nagual: Dawn Of The Dogmen

To Delilah —

Beware the Dogmen!

[signature]

Copyright © 2009 Frank Holes, Jr.
All rights reserved.
ISBN: 1-4392-4514-2
ISBN-13: 9781439245149

Visit www.booksurge.com to order additional copies.

Frank Holes, Jr.

NAGUAL: DAWN OF THE DOGMEN

2009

Nagual: Dawn Of The Dogmen

ACKNOWLEDGEMENTS PAGE/DISCLAIMER:

Once again, my deepest thanks go out to the following professionals who have aided the success of this novel: Craig Tollenaar, cover artist extraordinaire, who has designed the absolute best book covers in America (anytime I'm out and about, his work gets more compliments than I do); Daniel A. Van Beek, editor extraordinaire, who really turned this manuscript into a winner, despite the low body count (ha, ha); Sheryl Umulis, the real 'Cherry Lady' of Interlochen who shared both her fantastic cherry vinaigrette (order it at sixlugs.com) and her family's legends of Ogopogo; Eli Holes, my grandfather, who continues to read, re-read, proofread, and edited the first editions; John Reick and the crew at BookSurge who continue to make the publishing process so much fun; and Steve Cook, Traverse City DJ (and creator of the song "The Legend") who of course continues to be a good friend and inspiration for the Dogman stories.

The novel that follows is a work of fantasy and fiction. Although the many towns, cities, and camps surrounding Lake Ann and Interlochen are real places, the story location itself exists completely in the mind of the author. Any resemblance between the folks who live there and people who live in the real world is coincidental and unintended. There will surely be folks out there who try to follow the 'real' roads and highways in this story and find that I've played with the actual geography of Grand Traverse and Benzie Counties. Also please note that this novel is not based on any known Native American legends. I know that the sharing of real stories and legends of our Native American friends is a highly sensitive topic, and the only references to the various tribes contained herein are for historical accuracy and identification purposes only.

The Dogman, however, is very real to those who have seen or encountered the beast. After many years of sharing stories with dozens of actual witnesses, I've come to believe that something is undoubtedly out there in the north woods darkness. The tales I spin only pale in comparison to the many stories I've been told. Spend some time in Michigan's remote wilderness at night if you don't believe me.

Official *Nagual: Dawn of the Dogmen* information and merchandise can be found at our website:

http://www.dogman07.com

To Grandpa Charlie And Grandpa Eli,
To Grandma Annie Ma And Grandma Toni Ma,
And To All Of My Students, Past And Present.

The More You Know, The Harder It Is Not To Believe.

Imagine What Could Be Out There In The Darkness…

ALSO BY FRANK HOLES, JR.

Year of the Dogman
The Haunting of Sigma
The Longquist Adventures: Western Odyssey

http://www.mythmichigan.com

BOOK 1
December 1707

CHAPTER 1
The Watcher

The curtain of light snow continued to fall from the gray sky as the dark, shadowy figure plodded its way through the wilderness.

Seen from a distance through the flurry, its only resemblance to a humanoid was that it was walking on its two hind legs. And its gait wasn't exactly smooth—it leapt and lurched almost spastically through the drifts. Otherwise, one could have mistaken it for a monster or creature out of nightmare, an animal that had somehow found the evolutionary ladder and had fought its way up to a new stage in its development.

The creature continued its track, navigating through the thin, scrawny saplings, their wispy branches, like arms reaching to the sky in mock prayer, completely bare of leaves. Every now and then the creature would pass one of the larger trees and stop a few seconds to lean against the smooth bark. The snowdrifts within the forest were more compacted and not as deep as those out in the open country, but the going was slow and difficult nonetheless.

Snowflakes continued to whirl and crisscross in all directions from the light breeze. The strobe effect from the falling snow gave the world a surreal feel, like being in a dream. The flakes weren't exactly huge, but their sheer numbers made visibility difficult. Somewhere an owl hooted, a lonely call in the otherwise silent northern forest.

Not simply a trick of the light and the falling snow, the creature's hazy outline was actually due to its shaggy hair, which was only slightly matted down around the edges. The figure walked hunched over, its head hanging low and slightly tucked into its thick chest. Its arms constantly swung from side to side, keeping its balance as it moved forward.

***

However, to the watcher in the woods, crouching low and peering out between the cover of evergreen boughs, the moving shape did belong to a human. The watcher's instincts were very clear on that account. It may not have looked like it, but it was a man out there, struggling his way through the snow. It was a man indeed. The watcher knew it.

Night was quickly falling on the world. Darkness had already filled the voids and holes between the clumps of trees and along the backsides of snowy drifts and hills. The wind kicked up, and the world was momentarily lost in a white haze as millions of snowflakes skipped and danced along throughout the forest.

The man wouldn't be able to go on much longer. He was slowing, every movement becoming an effort. His progress would completely halt very soon.

The watcher didn't move. Stealth, silence and complete stillness were the only requirements. The watcher simply peered intently at the man moving through the drifts. Waiting. Watching.

***

The blanket of snow was already more than a foot deep, and it was only the traveling man's ingenuity that allowed him to continue moving forward. He only sank in a few inches because of his homemade snowshoes, which were really only large strips of thick, pliable tree bark, but they did the trick. These were lashed to his boots with thongs of leathery skin formerly belonging to a dead marsh rat, which had also served as the man's only bit of meat in the last two weeks. The rat hadn't turned out to be much of a meal, being rather thin and stringy, but the parts that couldn't be consumed were at least useful.

Rather flimsy and fragile, the tree-bark snowshoes might last a day under these harsh conditions. Some days, the traveling man had to stop two or three times to refashion his shoes. Luckily, the rat-thongs were not only tough but also reusable.

It was slow going, but pushing on was the only option.

Of course, he wasn't appropriately dressed for the conditions, but that was hardly his fault. He should have been back at Fort Mackinac more than a month earlier, warming himself by the hearth fire and enjoying a leisurely bowl of venison stew and perhaps a nip or two of firewater. He should have been back home counting his share of the fall's final fur trading expedition.

But he wasn't back home; he was here, shivering as he wiped the crust of ice that formed at the ends of his long and wispy moustache. The only parts of his body that really weren't freezing were his face and neck—they'd been covered with an ever-thickening beard that had been growing for several months now.

His hair, both on his pointed chin and up over his scalp, had turned a prematurely shade of white nearly overnight. And the color wasn't from the build up of snow, either.

From a distance, he appeared shaggy and animal-like, but it was mostly the overcoat he'd created from a coyote pelt. It was this homemade overcoat, stuffed with leaves, pine boughs, dead ferns, and anything else he could find for insulation, that kept him both somewhat dry and just warm enough to stay alive. Without the coat, he'd have expired weeks ago. The coyote had plagued him for three days. The first time he'd heard that lonesome canine howl, Pierre's blood froze and his breath caught in his chest. He'd been curled up beneath a massed pile of leaves for warmth, on the verge of another troublesome sleep. But he would awaken completely every time at that howl, as images of the blackest demons rushed back to the forefront of the Frenchman's mind. He'd never been able to forget that fateful night only two months ago. He'd never been able to forget the monster, its towering physique, its sharp fangs and claws, its glowing eyes. He'd never been able to rid his brain of the attack, the death of his companions, or the creature's roar of triumph. These memories troubled his sleep, and he'd often awake in the middle of the night, drenched with sweat, despite the cold temperatures.

It was a nightmare that never really dissipated with the dawn's light.

Though he did miss his companions—no, his friends—a great deal, he never regretted his flight that fateful night. He had run and run without a single thought of turning back.

What could he have done anyway, had he stayed? He'd have surely been killed, too. If their Algonquin guide, one of the toughest men he'd ever met, couldn't have bested the monster, what chance did the three fur traders stand?

So off he ran, blindly sprinting through the thick *Michigana* forest. The storm had raged around him, the heavy rain making every footfall a slick balancing act. Booms of thunder and streaks of lightning completed the nightmarish scene.

It was a miracle he was able to keep up the running pace that entire first night.

Adrenaline continued to pump through his body, making him nearly oblivious to the chilling winds that whipped through the woods. The bare skin of his face and hands was stung by the pelting rain and the poking branches of saplings. He gasped for breath, his lungs burning, yet he never stopped. There were no coherent thoughts in his mind, nothing but the animalistic flight response. Everything else took a back seat.

As the darkness dissipated the next morning, Pierre slowed to a walk. He would reach out and grasp the trees and branches, pulling himself forward, resting only momentarily. But every so often, when the wind would howl through the trees and the creature's snarling face resurfaced in his memory, he would take up his flight again, racing through the forest until he could no longer run. Time passed quickly during these endless periods of running and walking. But never once did he stop moving.

A few days later, physical exhaustion finally claimed him. He collapsed. Many hours later, upon awakening sore and tired, Pierre had a chance to examine the damage. A short hike to a small lake showed him a foreign face that was reflecting back toward him in the crisp, cold water. The cheeks and forehead were crossed with cuts and scratches, while the hair, formerly a deep shade of black, was now as gray-white as the storm clouds overhead. He barely recognized himself.

Realization hit home. The Frenchman had no idea where he was, only that he was fleeing from the most abhorrent creature he could have ever imagined.

More than once he had to wonder if it had ever happened at all, and if maybe there was some other explanation for his wandering in the wilderness. Perhaps it was all a dream. Perhaps he had never taken that last long trip south. Perhaps he'd never actually heard the ancient tale from the tribal chieftain. Perhaps he'd never dug deeply into that burial mound in the middle of a tributary of the great river, the *O-Wash-Ta-Nong*.

Perhaps he'd never awakened that awful demon from its resting place.

There was simply no way, however, he was going to stay in this country long enough to find out for sure. Even if it all had been a dream, he was still lost in the wilderness. Winter was fast approaching, and he was ill-equipped for survival.

Yet it had been no dream. The howling of the coyote was as real as the memories it conjured up. Pierre's brain refused rational thought at the sound of the wild canine in the night. Flight was the only response.

Normally, he was unafraid of anything in the wilderness. But his life was anything but normal now.

So he pressed on, tracking north as best as he could from the position of the ever-fleeing sun. Some days, when the thick cloud cover obscured the sun and the world was encased in gray, nothing but blind luck kept him going the right direction until he could discern the darkening eastern sky. On those days, once he was finally sure of his true direction, he ran until the world was nearly too dim to see. Then he'd find a place to hunker down and try to conserve warmth.

Finding food quickly became another major issue. After the attack on the river, all Pierre possessed were the clothes on his back. And those clothes were battered and slowly falling apart. He had no knife, no hatchet. The canoes and all of their provisions, overturned and scattered by the monster's attack, had undoubtedly floated off to be claimed by the great lake *Michigana*.

All the Frenchman carried were his years of wilderness experience and his wits. Both of these, however, like his health, were slipping away like sand through an hourglass. At this time of year, there was very little foraging to be done in the forest. The season was far too late for edible greenery of any sort, meaning that most animals had also made themselves scarce.

However, there were a few critters around, and Pierre fought against the ever-growing hunger in his belly, trying to remain patient. He used a sharp rock to chisel away the end of a sturdy stick, which then served as a makeshift spear. It took many, many tries to perfect the throw, but in the end, he did skewer a rabbit or another small animal at least once every other day. He had no way to cook his kill, but he didn't want a fire anyway. The convenience it brought was no trade-off for it potentially signaling his pursuer.

It was also difficult to hunt because he was constantly on the move. There was no way the Frenchman was going to remain in any one place for very long, not with the demon somewhere behind him. There was no telling how close or far away it might be. But he was taking no chances. The nightly howling seemed to constantly be closing in on him. The creature had tracked him once; it was most certainly tracking him again.

Pierre could only wonder how long it would take for the dog creature to catch up. Did he really think he could outrun it? His heart of hearts told him no, there was ultimately no escape. But his deepest instincts wouldn't let him stop trying. He'd keep running until he died of exposure to the elements, was caught and attacked by his pursuer, or managed to somehow find his way back home.

***

The howling had grown louder and more intense each of the next two nights after first hearing the coyote. The Frenchman had slept very little.

On the third night, he'd heard the creature's howl closing in on him, and just before dawn the fight began.

Pierre had taken to sleeping with his spear clutched tightly in his right hand. He'd also fashioned himself a long, sharp stone that he'd begun using as a knife. This he held tightly in his left hand. It was fortune indeed that his weapons were so close at hand.

The blackness of night had receded, giving way to the deepest violet of early morning. Shadowy shapes emerged from the total darkness, now given form by the tiniest bit of light.

Pierre had been desperately trying for some time to get even a few more minutes of precious sleep. When he heard the twig snap very nearby off to his right, his eyes flew open, though his body remained as still as death. Fingers that a year later would be full of arthritis now formed a death grip upon the two weapons.

He didn't move. He didn't even breathe.

Though the Frenchman couldn't see it, he sensed the creature's attack. Half a moment later, its powerful body sprang toward Pierre's hiding place at the base of a wide-spreading pine tree. As the boughs abruptly parted, the Frenchman jabbed his homemade knife upwards. The sharpened stone easily pierced the animal's body and Pierre was sprayed with warm blood. His cheek had been sliced open by one of the coyote's claws, but otherwise the creature's initial attack had failed. The coyote's shoulder then slammed into the pine's trunk, and Pierre was sure he heard a crack that probably didn't come from the tree.

The first onslaught lasted only a second. But the fight was now on. The coyote was a huge specimen, quite unlike its scrawny siblings and cousins. It had tracked its prey for several days to this dead end. Now it meant to finish off the man. However, pain and dizziness began to confuse the animal. Rather than ending the man's life in an instant, the coyote now found itself being attacked.

Pierre turned on the coyote, stabbing and beating it with his sharpened stone knife.

But the coyote wasn't done yet. Its jaws snapped over and over, teeth slashing like a steel trap. Its spittle flew in all directions. Sharp front claws tore at the man's clothing.

The Frenchman fell backward onto his butt in an attempt to avoid the animal's natural weapons. His momentum caused him to roll off to one side, and his body slipped out from beneath the branches. Pierre's maneuver gave the coyote an opportunity to spring again.

In such close quarters, Pierre's spear was far too awkward. However, once he was free from the confines of the pine boughs, the Frenchman could wield it as a far more effective weapon. He dropped the knife and held the spear with both hands.

A second later, the pine boughs erupted again as the coyote burst forth after its prey. Leaves and needles scattered in all directions, their shapes silhouetted in the early morning light.

Pierre's spear caught the animal right in the center of its chest. The coyote's weight and momentum did the rest, impaling itself along the shaft of the spear.

The Frenchman was pummeled backward, landing hard enough to knock the breath from his lungs, but he didn't lose his grip on the spear. The coyote soared overhead and hit the ground a few feet away. Its legs spasmed, clawed feet digging furrows into the soft ground while its jaws continued to snap in all directions, just a few inches from Pierre's head.

The man slipped into an exhausted unconsciousness. The beast's spasms finally ended as its lifeblood seeped out, soaking into the ground. Both man and beast lay flat on the soft forest floor, unmoving.

***

A few hours later Pierre was awaken by a beam of bright sunlight inching its way through the tree branches and crawling across his eyelids. He blinked a few times, pushing away the dregs of sleep. He propped himself up onto his sore elbows and looked around at the forest. It was a beautiful *Michigana* morning, the kind that belongs to early October rather than mid-December. As he took in the sight, Pierre first viewed what had been his burrow beneath the bushy pine. And when he turned the other way, he saw the huge coyote impaled upon the spear. It was then that he was able to piece together what had happened.

Though sore and stiff, he felt good. Really good. From the sun's position high above, the Frenchman knew he'd been asleep for quite some time. Obviously his body and mind needed the rest, though it had cost him several hours of travel time.

A cold breeze whistled its way through the forest, a stark contrast to the bright sunlight and the glimpses of the palette of blue sky behind the trees' leafless branches. It might look like an early October day, but this was just the eye of the storm that would become a dreadful and impending winter.

Pierre assessed himself and found no major damage, other than to his clothing. He then assessed the animal before him, and in due time, the coyote's skin became a coat.

***

That night, Pierre's dreams were haunted by memories. These were actual memories, not just terrifying images that flashed incoherently through his brain. Characters swam in and out, and though they were never clearly focused, their appearance told the story of his encounter with the demon.

First, the Frenchman saw an old, weathered Ottawa furrow his brow and purse his lips as he said bluntly, "We speak not of the dead hill." Immediately his face dissipated into the grassy mound that created an island in the middle of the river. The green grass sparkled in the sunlight. But a moment later, all turned to the purplish-black of night. The sun became the moon, glinting off the rippling water.

All went black in his dream. He heard one word reverberate through his mind. And it was odd, because it wasn't in French and it wasn't an Ottawa word he'd ever heard. But he understood it clearly, precisely.

Trespasser.

Yes, he was the trespasser. And now he had to pay for his transgression.

A bloodcurdling scream echoed through his brain, and Pierre knew right away it was that of his companion, Francois. They'd never found his body or any trace of him. And yet, Pierre knew what had taken him. He knew without a doubt.

He saw Etchemin, their trusty Algonquin guide, sling his hunting knife into the darkness at the edge of their campsite. He heard it embed itself up to the hilt within the dog creature's chest.

Another wizened, wrinkly face swam out of the darkness. Pierre couldn't remember his name (many small details were starting to slip from the Frenchman's memory, both while awake and while dreaming), but he was sure it was the great Ottawa chief, Gray Elk. This elder said, "The *Yam-Ko-Desh* attacked our villages, killed our people. They ate the flesh of those they killed, and they worshipped a god with a wolf's head."

The chief's face abruptly morphed into the visage Pierre knew only too well. He'd seen it clearly only twice in his life, and both times were only momentarily. But that face was burned into his memory. Pierre might be losing a lot of his memories, but this was one he could never forget. The new face was horrid, an evil blend of a human and a gigantic wild dog.

Adding to the horror of the dream, the dog creature narrowed its glowing yellow eyes, and a moment later, it smiled, revealing the blood-stained fangs below its muzzle. That was the worst part—the fact that it so closely resembled a human smile.

Trespasser.

That strange word from a strange language that he could somehow understand.

One last voice emerged before Pierre's mind went into deepest sleep. "Unless released, the evil of the *Yam-Ko-Desh* will never rise again."

***

Time passed eerily in this fashion. Days were spent running, hunting, trying to keep warm as the temperatures continued to fall. Some days he ate, some days he went hungry. Nights were plagued by dreams, voices, and of course, the face of the demon dog that walked like a man.

Storms continued to ravage the countryside, and Pierre's skin was constantly wrinkly and waterlogged. His wool trousers and shirt-jacket kept most of the cold wind out, but when they were soaked, he was miserable.

A week after killing the coyote, the first snow fell. It began as a very light dusting, tiny icicles that accompanied the rain. It stung the skin and melted on contact where it landed.

Now, two weeks later, the snow was a deep drift across the entire landscape.

The snow was, in many ways, a living being itself. It grew, it moved, and it completely ate up the color of the world. It would blow and bite at Pierre so ferociously that he seemed near to death more than a few times. But each time, the snow would pull back a bit, just a little, so that the human could struggle on. It was playing with the Frenchman, like a cat with a mouse—toying with him, teasing him, punishing him.

Every so often one of the Frenchman's hands would find its way to the necklace he wore, the only souvenir of the trip. It was this necklace that remained a stark reminder that this was no dream. It all did happen.

He was a bit disappointed that the necklace appeared to be missing several of the black jewels. They must have come loose and fallen off during his flight.

Maybe the creature stopped to pick them up, he mused. Somehow that made a strange kind of sense to the Frenchman. Maybe that's what has allowed me to escape. Certainly the creature should have overtaken me by now.

More than once, Pierre had thought of ripping off the accursed necklace and throwing it into the wilderness. But always there remained the slightest glimmer of hope. The necklace afforded him that.

***

More and more often as he fled, the Frenchman reached out to lean upon the bare tree trunks, pausing for longer periods at each. And his pace had slowed significantly. Already his feet were dragging through the snow rather than lifting clear. Arms once out to balance every step were drooping to the sides of his fur overcoat. His dark green knitted wool cap had been long lost, presumably in the battle with the beast who'd given him the coat.

Luckily, the harshest storms and bitter cold had yet to invade the land of *Michigana*. Some storms could dump a foot or more of damp snow upon the land in a single night. Some storms brought the winter rain that freezes, icing down the landscape. And yet other storms delivered pelting ice that burned the skin. The most frigid temperatures would hit in January or February when the frosty beauty of the brightest stars in the night sky belied the deadly cold. If he was caught out in those conditions, he would not survive. It wouldn't matter if he evaded his pursuer; he'd be dead and frozen, long before being caught.

He couldn't go on much farther.

Twenty feet. Rest. Ten feet more. Rest. What happened next was unavoidable.

The watcher's head twitched only the slightest bit as the Frenchman stumbled forward, reaching out desperately for the next tree. But his hands missed, the homemade snowshoes caught in the snow, and his body crashed into the drift below.

Crawling forward, Pierre tried his best to get back on his feet, but his struggle soon ended. He simply didn't have the strength.

Cautiously, the watcher broke cover and crept toward the man lying prone in the snow.

***

Pierre awoke in a strange environment. It was very dark around him, the only light coming from some distance away.

He blinked and then rubbed his eyes, trying to regain complete consciousness.

He didn't think he was dead, though he did feel rather comfortable.

If I'm not dead, then where am I? he asked himself.

Apparently his senses were still working. Pierre could smell something delicious cooking over the fire at the far end of the lodge. Of course, after many weeks of eating cold, raw meat and harsh scraps of frozen vegetation, anything bubbling away in a pot would smell great. It could have been dirty laundry for all he knew, but he believed it was probably a hearty stew of some sort.

He shivered, and that was when he noticed that his shirt was gone. And wrapped all around him were warm blankets and furs.

Then he tested each body part to see if it was working. Arms and legs stretched out, knuckles and neck cracked. He touched his fingers to his face and head, checking one last time to be sure that he was really alive.

Once his eyes adjusted to the dim lighting in the lodge, Pierre studied his surroundings. Slowly he turned his head one way and then the other, taking it all in. The lodge seemed about 30 feet long and possibly half that wide. Thick ribs, surely pliable saplings, rose from the ground and curved up overhead, meeting at a central beam that must have held up the roof. The walls were birch bark, sewn to the ribbing with what looked like thin, stringy tree roots. The birch bark sheets were overlapped, clearly designed to shed rain and snow down the outside, and thus keeping the interior as dry as possible.

The floor beneath him felt far too soft and warm to be the bare earth. The softness came from many layers of multicolored furs and blankets piled upon each other. As he pulled away a heavy, overlapping section, Pierre felt some sort of wooden platform beneath. It was much cooler down there, and he quickly replaced the insulating layers.

He was alone at the moment, but undoubtedly not for long, considering that dinner was boiling merrily away nearby. Pierre squinted into the distance, studying the cooking pot where wisps of steam escaped, rose in a cloud to the lodge's ceiling, and then condensed back into little streams of water droplets that chased each other down the sides of the birch bark.

Though he tried mightily to remember what had happened, his mind drew a blank. Pierre narrowed his eyes and bared his teeth behind his lips, concentrating with all of his might. But there was little there to recall. Bits and pieces of his journey flashed before his eyelids. *Running through the primeval forests. Storms soaking and numbing his body. Struggling through the snow. And all the time, hunger. And fear.*

Specific events might be beyond his recollection, but Pierre did know that, physically, he had been a mess. Someone had obviously taken great pains to tend to his broken and battered body. Despite the improvements, he still felt very weak, and just the process of sitting up, checking himself over, and looking around had tired him tremendously.

He closed his eyes to relax and took a few slow, deep breaths. He might be feeling a bit better, but he was still not in much shape to move about quite yet. The wonderful aroma of the stew in the pot drove him wild with hunger, though he wasn't sure he could muster the strength to crawl over there.

Just then, a shaft of light broke through the dim interior of the lodge as two dark silhouettes appeared in the doorway.

Pierre had had no contact with anyone for more than two months, and he had no idea what to expect from his hosts. He hoped that whoever had saved him was still friendly. He hoped they hadn't changed their minds about keeping him alive. He held his breath, waiting anxiously.

If they kill me, so be it, the Frenchman thought. *It'll be better than what the dog creature could do to me.*

Then the door flap slipped shut and the silhouettes sharpened into humans. The two pushed back the hoods of their long coats. Pierre exhaled, relieved.

They weren't warriors; they were women.

Both were dressed in a similar fashion, wearing long pants and coats stitched from leather. Tiny fronds dangled at the edges. At the cuffs and neckline, Pierre noticed the clothes were lined with a soft, tan fur. Beyond the clothing, the two women were as opposite as could be. The shorter one was ancient, her wrinkled face staring down unblinking. Her black hair, interspersed with many thin gray strands, was woven into two long braids that hung down her back. Her eyes were jet black, as emotionless as her face. She was stout, wide-shouldered, and despite the few feminine features in her face, she had the build of a man. This old woman even brooded over him with a silent authority.

The younger woman, however, was not only a head taller than her companion but also thin. Long, delicate fingers extended from slender wrists that protruded from the arms of her coat. Her hair was a chestnut brown, almost glowing a deep red from the firelight, and it hung in a single braid down her back. Pierre was struck by her simple beauty. It was too difficult to tell her eye color from the darkness inside the lodge, but Pierre could see these large, round eyes, like a doe's, were lively and sparkling. The young woman showed no signs of age—she could have been anywhere between 16 and 30.

In a very graceful manner, this younger woman glided past the Frenchman and over to the cooking fire. He watched as she ladled a bowl of thick liquid from the stewpot and brought it to him. Steam rose from the bowl, the aroma too much for Pierre to resist. He greedily drank it down despite burning his tongue, mouth, and throat.

She refilled the bowl as soon as it was emptied. This time she also brought him a bowl of cold, clear water. Both disappeared in a matter of seconds.

"A powerful hunger like yours is a good sight," the young woman spoke to him in French. "It is good to see you are recovering your strength."

Astonished, Pierre's eyes widened. "You speak French?" He was a bit surprised by the rasp in his own voice.

"Yes," the young woman answered. "But I am the only one in our village who can do so. My name is *Say-Too-Dee*, which means 'Red Feather' in your language. You are a guest here in my grandmother's lodge."

"How did I get here?" Pierre asked, again hardly recognizing his own voice. He'd been alone so long, he wondered how long it had been since he'd actually spoken aloud. Weeks? Months?

"I watched you struggling through the storm," the young woman replied, very matter-of-factly. "I was very curious as to why a White Skin would be so far from his own village in the depths of winter.

"I watched you carefully, as we are taught to avoid intruders. But you were in desperate need. I knew that without help you would reach the Heart of Heaven well before Grandfather Moon rose above the trees. Your skin was as cold and blue as the *Wahbekanetta*."

"What is the *Wahbekanetta*?" Pierre asked. It was a word that sounded as if it was French but he was unfamiliar with it.

"*Wahbekana* is the goddess of the lakes," Red Feather explained. "Our village lies between the *Wahbekanetta* and *Wahbekaness*, the twin lakes where she makes her home. We offer gifts of flowers, carefully pressed last summer, to appease *Wahbekana*. We ask for her blessings to survive the winter and return life to our land in the spring.

"It is my duty to offer this gift before the full moon rises. I was returning to my village when our paths crossed." She touched the skin below her throat with her open palm and then held this hand out to the Frenchman. "There was no time to call for help from my village. So I lashed you to a downed pine branch and pulled you here."

"How far did you have to pull me?" he asked incredulously.

Red Feather thought for a moment, then replied, "I had you here safely before Grandfather Moon even showed his full face. You were only a couple of bird flights away from our village."

Pierre stared at the women, his mouth hanging open, completely amazed. This woman couldn't have weighed more than a hundred pounds, and yet she had the strength to drag him through the thick snow to safety. Quickly, too. His last memory had been struggling through the storm in the twilight. That meant she'd pulled him quite a distance in an hour's time or less. *And in the middle of a snowstorm, too.*

"I see you are doubtful," she smiled again at him, tilting her chin upward in pride. "The Omeena women are strong. Unlike the families of the White Skins, here it the woman's role to run each *waginogan*, our word for the family lodge. My grandmother, *Wa-Kama*," she said, now introducing her shorter, wrinkled companion, "which means 'Spring Mother' in your language, is also the chieftain of our village. My medicine is strong, and she has trained me since I was very young. But she has the greatest power in the tribe, and only together could we bring you back from the Heart of Heaven."

Death, she means, thought Pierre. *They saved me from death.*

It was all so very strange to the Frenchman. He'd never head of a matriarchal society. He tried unsuccessfully to imagine a woman being the head of the tribe. He wondered where the other members of the family were.

The two women continued to stare down at him in silence.

Pierre was still unsure whether or not they were completely friendly. Sure they saved him, but was there some purpose behind it other than simply generosity? The silence was troubling him. He tried again to make conversation. "This lodge is quite large for just you and your grandmother," he noted.

Red Feather, now kneeling at the feet of her grandmother, glanced over at him. "The other members of our *waginogan* are staying in neighboring lodges while you are here. They don't trust strangers, and most don't approve of you staying here with us. They will avoid us while you are here."

Pierre felt his face flush as he realized the inconvenience his presence created. He also realized these two women were sticking their necks out for him, that they were caring for him without support from anyone else in the tribe.

Then the younger woman smiled at him, a genuine flash of warmth and friendliness. Even in the dim light of the lodge, Pierre realized she was very beautiful. He realized he was staring too long at her, and turned his eyes away in embarrassment.

Unabashed, Red Feather said to him, "I see you are uneasy. Please, settle your heart. You are welcome here. No one will interrupt your recovery. You are safe here with us."

Pierre returned his gaze to the two women, the younger one with the grand smile and the elder who stood looking down upon him stone-faced. Indeed, he felt welcome here in the warm lodge. But in the deepest recesses of his mind, he wondered how safe he was. How safe could he really be with a ghastly specter following his trail? How safe was anybody around him?

"Normally our tribe avoids the White Skins whenever possible. Our only dealings with them are when they wish to trade with us. There is very little the White Skins have that we need or want. But the men of our village are excellent hunters, and we have many furs and skins that the White Skins want. Our elders disapprove of this, but we know it is inevitable."

Red Feather dropped her eyes for the briefest moment, then returned them to the Frenchman. "I feel the paths of the Omeena and the White Skins will merge, it is only a matter of time. I only hope the Omeena will be able to survive the change that is coming to our land. I fear for us."

Pierre cocked his head. "I've never heard of the Omeena," he said slowly to her.

The corners of her mouth turned up in a little grin. "That is a good thing," she said. "It is better to have as few contacts with the White Skins as possible. We will tell you more later. For now, you must rest and recover."

***

Many days passed as Pierre regained his strength. The chills and night sweats subsided. However, he was not allowed to leave the lodge, on Wa-Kama's orders. He wasn't sure he really wanted to anyway. On the couple of rare occasions when he'd peeked his head outside, he was met with distrustful, accusing stares from the villagers.

Very soon he'd have to move on. He was sure he'd overstayed his welcome in the village.

There was one face in the crowd, however, that didn't stare back with hostility. One young face saw a glimpse of Pierre's necklace. In the briefest of moments, this young man's eyes locked on the glint of the jewels, and he felt them call out to him. The mind behind that young face yearned to possess the claw-shaped jewels, all to himself.

***

When Pierre awoke, it was very dark. The cooking fire had burned down to bright red coals that glowed in the distance. He'd had that nightmarish series of memories again, except this time the final words spoken by Gray Elk were followed by the visage of the creature, its glowing yellow eyes boring deeply into the Frenchman's soul. The last image he saw was the dog creature reaching out for him, its muzzle curling up in what appeared to be an evil smile.

That was when Pierre bolted upright, breathless, with beads of sweat popping out on his forehead. His hands were tightly gripping the blankets that still encircled him.

Wa-Kama and Red Feather were sitting crossed-legged a few feet away. They were looking at him intently. Then the old woman spoke in a low, whispering voice.

Red Feather translated. "She says it is the *O-gano-powah-go* you've seen. She can tell because you carry its *zemi*."

Pierre gave her a confused look.

"The *zemi* around your neck," the younger woman said, pointing at the claw-shaped jewels that hung on Pierre's necklace.

Immediately, the Frenchman's right hand rose and covered the necklace. He could feel its warmth beneath his fingers, as if the clawed jewels were radiating their own heat.

Pierre stared back into the blackness of both women's eyes. Gulping, he quietly asked, "What is the *O-gano-powah-go?*" He was pretty sure of her answer before she gave it.

"It is the dog who walks as a man," said Red Feather without translation from her grandmother. "It is but one type of *Nagual*, what you would call a 'skin-walker,' an ancient demon from the world beyond." Her arm rose and made a graceful curve around the room and overhead.

The old woman held up her hand and continued on as Red Feather fell silent. At one point, Pierre tilted his head as he recognized a word that sounded much like *Yam-Ko-Desh*, which he'd heard over and over in his nightmares. Only the old woman had said *Ya-May-Go-Dash.* He wondered if this was similar to the tribal name he'd learned at the Ottawa council so long ago.

Red Feather again translated. "She wonders where you acquired the *zemi* of the *O-gano-powah-go*. She knows it comes from the *Ya-May-Go-Dash*, and its emergence here in our peaceful country is indeed a frightful omen."

Pierre took a deep breath before answering. "My companions and I were guests of the Ottawa far to the south. We were trading furs with them before winter set in. Gray Elk, their great chief, told us the *Yam-Ko-Desh* was a group of invading Indians who belonged to a wolf cult. He said they believed their warriors could take on the personage of a wolf when in battle."

Red Feather passed this on to her grandmother who nodded and spoke in return. The young woman listened carefully for a long time and then turned to speak to the Frenchman.

"She says Gray Elk did not tell you the entire story. She knows the story because it has been passed down through many generations of the Omeena, just as it has been passed down through many generations of the Ottawa.

"The *Ya-May-Go-Dash* was much more than a wolf cult. They may have looked like humans on the outside, but beneath the skin, they were inhabited by demons. They'd traded their souls for unnatural and evil powers.

"They did invade our *Michigana* land in the time long past. At one time, they were just evil humans. Their tribe slaughtered entire villages as sacrifices to their wolf god. These sacrifices fueled the black magic of their *Naymago*, their dark and evil chieftains.

"Only the deepest, most powerful black magic could open a portal between our world and the empty space beyond. And through this portal came the *Nagual*, the skin-walkers, the demons who inhabited the bodies of the *Ya-May-Go-Dash*, changing them into beasts that were neither human nor animal. The human's soul went into the blackness and the demon took its place here in our world."

"But there's no such thing as magic or other worlds," Pierre said. Yet in the deep reaches of his mind, he had to question such a statement. How else could he explain the encounter he'd had at the burial mound and the attack on his companions? His mind split between rational thought and his irrational experience, a rift that would, over time, end up destroying his sanity.

Red Feather smiled knowingly at him. Her long eyelashes blinked several times over her wide eyes. "Of course there is. All tribes throughout history have used magic. We humans were born of magic, though most of us have forgotten how to bring it forth from the world around us anymore.

"The *Nagual* are creatures of the darkest magic. They have inhabited the darkness longer than humans have inhabited the earth. Our oldest legends tell of tribes that have been tempted by these demons' promise of power. Great wars were fought between the skin-walkers and the ancient people of many different tribes. Only when united could our ancestors defeat the might of the skin-walkers."

Pierre was intrigued by the story, but despite his encounter with the creature, he wasn't ready to believe in magic. Or maybe he was. His rational side, though crumbling, tried desperately for a reprieve. He'd need proof to really believe Red Feather's words. "Even if those stories were true, that was long, long ago. And they're just legends, right? Surely there isn't any magic left in the world."

A few seconds after he finished speaking, the old woman reached out with one wizened, wrinkled hand and deftly plucked the red feather from her granddaughter's hair. Pierre watched intently as the old woman held her other hand flat, palm side up. The skin was crisscrossed with deep lines. She stood the feather upright and carefully slid her fingers up its blade until they were an inch above it. The tips of her fingers and thumb were pinched together, pointing down at the feather that stood straight up on its own, balancing on her wrinkly hand.

Then, to Pierre's astonishment, she spread her fingers wide and the feather instantly changed into a tall flame. The old woman never even flinched. There were no burn marks on her skin, no sign that the mysterious flame affected her in the least.

The Frenchman could see the reflection of the narrow tongue of flame in both women's eyes.

Red Feather's grandmother suddenly snapped her open palm shut into a fist, and the flame disappeared. When she slowly opened the fist again, a tiny, red bird appeared. It looked around, chirped, and then in one smooth motion, circled up and out of the hole in the lodge's roof.

Pierre's mouth gaped open, awestruck by what he'd seen.

"You see?" the young woman asked quietly and confidently, "Magic still exists. There are just very few left who know how to use it."

Once again, Wa-Kama spoke, this time much more agitated and with emotion. Her hands waved back and forth, in a rather animated fashion.

"She says you must not allow the *O-gano-powah-go* to reclaim its *zemi*. The more pieces of the *zemi* it possesses, the more powerful it becomes."

"What would happen if the *O-gano-powah-go* were to get them all back?" Pierre asked timidly. Again, he felt he knew the answer already.

Both Wa-Kama and Red Feather looked at him gravely before the younger woman spoke. "It could bring forth the end of the world as we know it."

***

The Frenchman's feeling of safety here in the village was only a facade. Sure, his health had returned, but his dreams were still disturbed by images of the monster. He continued to awake every night screaming from a horrific nightmare.

And the nightmares were changing for the worse. Instead of just the awful memories, Pierre was now plagued with long, epic dreams where he relived the attacks. He saw the burial mound, the way the earth pulled at him and tried to bury him with the relics. He saw the dog demon lunge at him, felt the bitter cold as its ghost entered his body. He heard the awful screams of his friend Francois in the blackness of their campsite. He relived the frantic search that revealed no clues as to his friend's whereabouts.

But most vividly, he remembered the last attack, more details surfacing. Etchemin, their Algonquin guide, had buried his tomahawk in the creature's shoulder and his long hunting knife up to its hilt in the creature's chest. And yet, the dog demon, this *Nagual*, didn't die.

Pierre remembered running off at full speed into the thick forest, hearing the creature's howling mingled with the death screams of his companions and friends far behind.

Some nights, he even dreamed he was the creature. These were surreal experiences, as if he were looking through a single spyglass. And yet everything was tinted with a yellowish luminosity.

Within the central circle of vision, all was clear, surprisingly detailed even from great distances. But all around the edges, his vision was blurred. On occasion, he'd glimpse a part of a clawed hand or a fur-covered forearm. Sometimes, he could tell when the creature leapt over streams or clung to the trunks of wide trees, its claws easily buried in the bark.

It was he who was the creature, running through the wilderness. Sickened, he'd watch as it would occasionally catch and rip apart an animal. And always, he thought the dog demon was looking for something, following a trail that the human could almost even see himself in his dreams.

Upon awakening, Pierre knew of course what the Dogman was trailing.

He knew with all of his being that the monster was tracking him.

However, he had no idea how far away it was. It could be miles away, or it could be very close. Pierre also knew that if the demon wanted him, it would not wait patiently for him to leave the village; it would come right in after him.

The Frenchman knew he had to move on fairly soon.

And he was pretty sure the other members of the Omeena tribe were just as anxious to be rid of him.

**

Pierre came out of one of these horrible nightmares to see a figure standing over him. But it wasn't Red Feather or Wa-Kama. He wasn't used to seeing anyone else come in or out of the *waginogan.* This was a young man, not much more than a child and certainly not quite yet an adult. He looked down at the Frenchman with unblinking, black eyes.

And yet, this young warrior wasn't looking at Pierre, at least not directly. His gaze was fixed on the *zemi* around Pierre's neck.

Carefully, the young Omeena reached out his hand and pointed at the black jewels. Then he finally looked Pierre in the eyes. He began to rattle off something in his own language, but the Frenchman stopped him short, shaking his head. The young man didn't have to say it; Pierre knew exactly what he wanted.

Pierre couldn't help but wonder where Red Feather and Wa-Kama were. They were in the *waginogan* often, even sleeping at the other end of the lodge. Either they had left the *waginogan* early or he was sleeping late. Considering his epic dreams, it was probably him sleeping in.

The young Omeena held up four fingers, indicating his desire to obtain just four of the precious jewels. Without thinking, Pierre raised his left hand up to cover the necklace.

Scowling, the young man reached into a small pouch he produced from inside his coat. Out of the pouch he brought a bracelet made with shells, a wooden carving of what appeared to be a bear, and several other trinkets.

None of these items was worth anything to Pierre, so he shook his head and crossed his hands out in front of his bare chest. *No, the necklace is worth far more than this junk*, he thought.

The young Omeena tried again, dropping down to his knees on the many blankets and skins that made up the lodge's floor. This time, he held up each of his items, turning them one way and then another, describing the obvious merits of each in his own language. But Pierre wasn't interested.

Scowling again, the young man rocked back on his haunches and stared at the Frenchman. Then, he reached into the folds of his warm clothing and brought out a long hunting knife.

Pierre gulped, knowing he was in a poor position. He had no weapons to defend himself, and though he was stronger now than before, he didn't think he could overpower this young man, even if he wasn't quite an adult. Red Feather and Wa-Kama were the only two in the village who were sympathetic to him, so Pierre knew that he couldn't cry out for help or even go racing out of the lodge.

With the knife in one hand, the young Omeena again gestured with four fingers of his other hand. This time he smiled, knowing he had the advantage.

With no other choice, Pierre began to pull the necklace up over his head. Luckily, the door flap then opened, spilling daylight into the *waginogan*.

Red Feather's loud, commanding voice was a contrast to the quiet, conversational tones she used with Pierre when they talked. She shouted harshly at the young man in her own language. The young Omeena took one last, squinted yet

31

malevolent look at the Frenchman before scurrying out of the *waginogan.*

"Have you been hurt?" she asked Pierre when the door flap had dropped back into place and the lodge returned to its shadowy self.

"I am fine," he replied, though he was sure Red Feather could see he was shaken. Near-death experiences may have happened to him often in recent months, but he never really became used to them.

"That is Laughing Quail, my own younger brother. He is always up to mischief. It is not good that he shows interest in your *zemi,*" she explained, her voice trailing off. "I was afraid of this."

Pierre looked up at Red Feather. Her large, beautiful eyes were full of worry. "I'm no longer safe here, am I?" he said, more a statement than a question.

Red Feather exhaled deeply. "You will need to go soon. Wa-Kama and I can protect you for another day or two, but I'm afraid you will have to leave our village. I am afraid Laughing Quail will stir up trouble. It will be best for all if you can leave soon."

***

A day later, Pierre left the Omeena village behind and made his way through the snow. The going was much easier with Omeena snowshoes. These real, handcrafted snowshoes were going to get him much farther than the ones he'd made from tree bark.

He tried to concentrate on the journey ahead. He was well supplied by Red Feather, to whom he owed his life. His body's warmth was now further insulated by many layers of warm clothing, and he carried pouches laden with dried food. He was well equipped with new snowshoes, a bone knife, and a stone-headed tomahawk. These were the best tools an explorer could ask for to make the journey home.

Red Feather was the only Omeena to see him off. Most of the rest of the tribe had hung back, just barely out of sight behind lodges and trees. Pierre could see them poking their faces out to make sure he was truly leaving.

It was too bad the tribe shunned visitors, especially the White Skins, he thought. *This was one place I could have settled down.* He thought again of Red Feather's simple beauty, the way she selflessly cared for him and nursed him back to health. He liked her strong character, the way she stood up for him despite what the others thought. *Maybe I'll find a way to come back this way again some day,* he thought.

Several hours passed since leaving the village, and the sun was already heading back toward the southwest. It was a great day to travel. The snow sparkled in the sunlight. Though the sky was clear and blue, he knew time was of the essence. Winter wasn't entirely over; it was just taking a short break. And the fort at Mackinac was still a long way off.

Using the sun as his guide, Pierre made his way as close to a northerly route as possible. Occasionally he had to detour around a thick grove of trees or what he believed might be a snow-covered pond. Mostly he was able to keep a fairly straight, unimpeded course.

But then, coming around a long line of tightly packed fir trees, the Frenchman stopped. About 50 feet ahead of him, there was a man standing in his way. Pierre waited, watching this guardian.

Trespasser, he heard his mind say.

Since Pierre wasn't moving forward, the man ahead of him chose to close the distance. Traversing well on snowshoes, the man blocked the path easily, and in no time, the two were only a few feet from one another. Pierre studied him closely. He was bundled beneath several layers of warm clothing. When the light breeze died down, the man pulled back his hood.

It was Laughing Quail, the young Omeena man with whom he'd wrestled a few nights earlier! Somehow, he'd circled around and ahead of the Frenchman.

The young man adamantly held up four fingers and pointed his spear at the Frenchman. He wasn't going to budge. He obviously wanted four of the clawed jewels, the same deal he was unable to get in Wa-Kama's *waginogan*. His clear, black eyes stared deeply, unblinking.

Pierre had his knife close at hand, but his tomahawk was inaccessible. Even if he could get it out, however, he knew the young warrior had the advantage. A good spear in well-trained hands was a tremendous weapon. Trying to pull out his own weapon would only get him killed. His best bet was to make a trade. He didn't want to, but it had to be done.

As an experienced fur trader, Pierre knew how to bargain with the native tribesmen even when there was a complete language barrier. He first spread his arms wide, palms open. Then, he pulled them together to form a bowl with his thumbs pointed upward. He slowly moved his hands toward the young man, indicating his part in the trade. Then Pierre pulled his hands back and pointed all of his fingers at his own chest. This displayed they would be bargaining with both sides expecting a trade.

The demand could have been for the entire necklace. At least the young warrior was willing to trade for just a couple of the jewels.

Carefully, Pierre pulled the fragile necklace out from under the many warm skins and then over his head. There were less than a dozen of the pointed, claw-shaped jewels left. A few of the jewels had been lost during his journey, and the rawhide thong showed several knots where Pierre had tied it back together. Four of these jewels then slipped off the thong and fell into his hand. Their shiny, black surfaces seemed to glow despite the brightness of the snowy field around them.

The young man's eyes widened and a faint smile turned the corners of his mouth upward. Unlike Red Feather and Wa-Kama, this young Omeena man was very interested in treasures.

Holding out his spear in one hand, the young warrior opened one hand, palm up.

Now it was Pierre's turn. He closed his fist around the jewels and held his other hand up, palm out. Pierre pointed to his mouth, and then pointed at the pouch hanging at the young man's waist. There really wasn't anything else the warrior had, other than his coat, spear, and snowshoes, and really, Pierre had those items already. However, there was always a need for more food.

The young warrior was taken aback for a moment. Then he bowed, grimacing a little to the trade.

The two kindly exchanged the clawed jewels for the bag of dried meat. The Omeena man, devoid of any anger and now fascinated by his half of the trade, simply walked right past the Frenchman as if he didn't exist. Pierre turned and watched him, the young warrior's snowshoes stepping lightly into the path Pierre had previously made, leading back to the Omeena village.

He hated that four of his precious jewels were now gone. Pierre reached his hand up and his fingers counted the remaining jewels. Just 7 jewels were left out of the original 16 that comprised the necklace. But all things considered, it was a small price to pay for his life. The two women at the village had asked for nothing in return; they'd expected no payment for the aid they had provided. And Pierre did receive another pouch of food for his journey. In the scarcity of winter, food was vital. He couldn't eat the jewels.

The business of trading done, Pierre started his northward journey again. He wasn't exactly pleased by the transaction, but there was really little he could do about it. A few hours later, as twilight crept upon the land, the howling wind erased the Frenchman's tracks completely.

CHAPTER 2
Dawn of the Dogmen

As the sparkling winter sun sank quickly to the horizon and the long shadows overtook the world, Pierre found an excellent spot to camp. Half a dozen large oaks made a perfect wind screen, and several low and wide pines provided a bit of cover overhead.

The Frenchman dug down into the packed snow and then pushed it up several feet, forming walls around his little refuge. When he was done, he had just enough space to curl into and protect himself from the elements. He then gathered a pile of kindling and firewood to burn through the night. Using supplies provided by Red Feather, he built a small fire and nibbled on dried jerky and fruits just as the winds began to howl through the cold forest. In his dugout, Pierre was protected and even felt warm.

On the part of his journey that ended at the Omeena village, he would never have thought of a fire. Of course at that time, he'd had nothing to start a fire with anyway. However, since leaving the village, he'd lit a small fire each night. His very survival in this deepening winter depended upon the heat now. At this point, it became a necessity, even if he did worry that it might attract his pursuer. If the Dogman found him cold and frozen, it wouldn't matter anyway.

Somehow, though, Pierre felt he was outdistancing the creature. He had no idea how he could feel this, and yet he knew it to be true. He could feel the creature pursuing him in this world was further away. It wasn't that the Dogman wasn't still tracking him; it had been detained. In fact, Pierre had the ungrounded suspicion that the creature might even be hibernating. *It hasn't gone away*, he thought. *Not totally. But I don't think it's right behind me anymore.*

Again, he had nothing to base this on, just a deep seated intuition.

Even the necklace had gone silent. It simply rested against his skin, lying there cold, hard, and sharp. Pierre had once thought it held some sort of life itself, but now it was just dead. *Or playing dead*, he thought, his fingers absently touching the smooth surface of one gem-claw. *Are you just waiting for the right time?* he silently asked it. *Are you and the demon both just waiting, resting, gathering your strength? I do wonder.*

***

That night Pierre dreamed, a disturbing and cataclysmic vision of the distant past.

But it was more than the jumbled, often confusing group of images that had haunted him for months.

It was a marathon of a dream, the kind that lasts the entire night, drawing you deeper and deeper into the subconscious realms. Some of the ancient ones, the world's greatest storytellers, might have said such a dream could span nights or even years in depth and complexity. It might have been simply a hallucination caused by stress and the horrific tales and experiences that inhabited Pierre's life these past few months. And yet it seemed to have been so much more.

Displayed on the canvas of the Frenchman's dreamy mind, a page from the story of the *Nagual* unfolded. It was a story far beyond the telling of an old Omeena woman or an aging

Ottawa chief. It was something that had to be seen to be believed.

From the sea of darkness in his mind, Pierre saw the land slowly emerge. It was as if existence was created before his very eyes, the eyes of his dream world. Light, though muted, divided the darkness and the sun slowly emerged in the cloudy sky. The land separated from the firmament above, and then the earth itself took on the texture of hills, plains, mountains, and valleys.

And yet, as the details sharpened, he realized the sky and land never really grew any lighter. The world was shrouded in darkness, almost a haze. It was like looking through a dirty window at the twilight beyond.

Thick strata of clouds wove a tapestry of muted color across the sky. Here and there maroon and magenta splashed against a royal velvet of indigo and violet. And these wisps contrasted with the deepest gray and charcoal. It was an angry and unsettled sky, ready and waiting for the right signal to pour forth its malevolence upon the world below.

Somehow, however, despite the constant barrage of the cloud blankets, the sun's golden orb maintained its majestic splendor.

But even that brilliance from the sun couldn't lift the haze that enshrouded the world below. Everything was still far too dark, too dim.

The Frenchman's vantage point was rather high above the earth, from where he could see everything, but he felt no fear whatsoever. He was neither standing upon a rocky precipice nor clinging to the limbs of the tallest tree. Pierre could not fathom the sensation of floating in space, and his mind could only insist that he was seeing the world as if from the eyes of a bird. And this only mystified him even more.

Stretching from horizon to horizon, the world below was a matching piece to the lusterless patchwork of clouds above. Covering most of the land, Pierre could see, was a vast plain, broad and flat in all directions, the dull beige of its grasses and the gray-green of its low mosses only broken occasionally by a drab, green speck that was surely a stunted tree or shrub.

At the far right of the great plain, the land rose slowly and steadily into the jagged teeth of a mountain chain. Even from this distance Pierre could see they weren't gigantic or majestic like those in his native France. But they were mountains, nonetheless, and those were relatively unheard of here in the *Michigana* territory. He could tell that it must be springtime, because the tips of the mountain peaks glimmered, showing only the remnants of the winter snow.

To the far left, a great forest, thick with age, stretched from the edge of the plain to the far horizon. The trees, bathed in the strange negative light of the world, only dimly resembled their normal selves. Occasionally a flock of birds, like tiny black dots from this distance, would rise up like a plume of smoke, circle and chase each other for a few seconds, and then dive back below.

It was cold, and the chilling sensation in this dream state was rather new to the Frenchman. He'd never remembered his senses triggered in a dream or nightmare before. His emotions, yes, but never his senses. A cold breeze sent chills through the body he inhabited in the dream.

As he stared into the deep bluish-gray of the mountains in the distance, a dark shadow appeared at the crest of the lowest foothills. For a few seconds, this shadow only peeked over the low rises of land. Soon, however, it steadily began spreading its way toward the valley floor, like wine spilled from a goblet. Or blood pouring from a wound.

Pierre's view changed, and he felt the cool wind brush his face as he swooped down and forward, traversing the great plain. The land rushed past him in a blur. It was impossible to determine the distance at which he flew above the earth. Only once did he look down, and the distorted view of grass and shrub nearly made him dizzy.

Again, he was amazed by the sensations he was feeling. This was no ordinary dream—it was more of an out-of-body experience. And it was as frightening as it was exhilarating.

He returned his gaze forward and realized he'd gone a long way in a very short time. The mountains, once small in the distance, had grown before his eyes, doubling then tripling in size, until that bluish-gray came into focus. But it wasn't earth and stone the Frenchman saw. Either Pierre was no longer in the *Michigana* country or he'd slipped somewhere through time to an age when ice covered much of the world. The blue-violet and gray was the reflection of the cloudy sky in the great ice sheet of a gigantic glacier covering the land! And it wasn't springtime—this wasn't snow melting in anticipation of a coming summer. It would never be summer in these men's lifetimes. This climate, this age, was on the very edge of a permanent winter.

The foothills of ice, packed as tightly and solid as any stone mountain, rushed up to meet him. It was then that he saw the dark shadow for what it really was.

Running at full speed down the hillsides was a massive army, so tightly packed together that from a distance it took on the visage of a single, spreading mass. The closer Pierre came, the more details he picked up. The army was comprised of humans whose skin was even darker than that of the natives with whom he so often traded. And over this deep, brown skin each warrior wore clothing of the blackest pitch.

Before he could see the warriors in closer detail, Pierre rose higher above the army. He felt he had no control over the flight, only the ability to look around. As he turned his view back downward, he saw the great clouds of dust and chaff that rose up around the warriors, especially those behind the front lines. If he was indeed seeing the world from the eyes of a bird, Pierre was thankful that this bird's instincts kept it well above the chaos below.

Pierre banked to the right and came across the army again, much lower this time from the flank. More details became visible. The warriors' skin was painted in fierce black and red patterns. Circles, interrupted with jagged lines, crisscrossed the men's bodies where the skin showed. These patterns seemed almost carved into the skin of these humans, perhaps even burned in.

Encircling each warrior's neck was a thong on which was strung anywhere from three to five or more sharply pointed jewels. To the Frenchman, these necklaces were far too familiar. He had one of his own, didn't he?

A *zemi*. That's what the old woman called it, a *zemi*.

But it was the clothing that was the most fearsome aspect of the warriors. Strapped to the back, shoulders, and chest of each man was the pelt of a great, black wolf. At the very top, a wolf's head adorned each warrior's head like a helmet. The wolf's muzzle protruded above and beyond each man's forehead, the ears pointed back from the great rush of air as they ran. Between the jaws of the wolf's head peered a face, entirely painted black. Only the whites of the eyes provided any sense of humanity.

This fearsome army, numbering in the thousands, tirelessly raced across the ground, mindless of the various fragments of ice, hard and dark as real stones, which lay scattered over the glacier. Finally reaching the plain, the front ranks of the warriors completely trampled the mosses and long, thin blades of grass underfoot.

The Frenchman again turned and rose above the army, this time looking to its origins at the foothills. The last ranks of the dark warriors left the sanctuary of the natural folds of land and started down toward the plain.

Behind them, Pierre could see their leader. From past experience, Pierre guessed that this was a great medicine-man, judging by the plumes of long, deep black feathers that adorned his head gear. He was a giant of a man, seeming to be nearly twice the size of any warrior Pierre had seen in the army that had passed him. Massive muscles rippled along the skin of his arms and legs. He was dressed in similar fashion to the warriors. His skin was black and also painted with those strange red symbols. Yet unlike the simple wolf heads and hides worn by the warriors, their leader's garb was greater and far more elaborate.

The creature who'd reluctantly given its skin to protect this leader had been a mighty beast indeed. In shape and structure, it did resemble a gigantic canine, but its own head was two or three times the size of those the warriors wore. This monster had a long muzzle and pointed ears like the others, but that was where the similarities ended. Unlike any creature Pierre had ever seen, this one had had four long saber-like teeth protruding from the muzzle, two from the top and two from the bottom. These monstrous fangs curved down to form a cage around the sorcerer's face.

And around his neck, just like those worn by the warriors, was situated a necklace, though his must have been adorned with two dozen or more of the claw-shaped black jewels. The claws on this necklace were easily the length of a man's hand from palm to fingertip. Pierre guessed that these were representative of the actual claws belonging to the beast whose pelt covered the head and shoulders of the medicine-man.

Undoubtedly the commander of this army, the gigantic chieftain rode into battle in an elaborate two-wheeled cart that was pulled by a pair of enormous creatures of a kind Pierre had never seen or even imagined before. At the great humped shoulder, each beast was taller than a man, again as wide, and twice as long. These beasts rumbled forward on four fur-covered legs, each as thick as an oak tree. Beneath the long, stringy dark-gray fur Pierre could see the animals' skin, which had the look of overlapping plates of dull armor, though he was pretty sure it was constructed using a hard leather rather than made of metal. The strands of fur were so long on the beasts' bellies and throats that these nearly touched the ground several feet below.

But the most distinguishing feature of these massive creatures was their heads. Whereas the rest of their bodies were covered in fur, their bald heads, smooth and hard as boulders washed along the sea, provided a complete contrast. In fact, the only hair visible on their faces was the bushy brows above the beasts' small, beady eyes. And at the front of their snub-nosed muzzles was extended a wide, curving black horn about the length of a grown-man's arm. At its base, the horn was wider than a man's thigh, and it tapered upward to a sharp point. Though Pierre had never in his life imagined such an odd monstrosity, he knew such a weapon at the creature's forefront was useful for one thing—bringing death to anything that stood in its way.

These two massive beasts easily towed the chieftain's cart at a pace akin to a man jogging. Every now and then one of the creatures would grunt and slam its head and horn into the other, which would respond with a deep bellow, foamy spittle flying in all directions. The commander didn't even look at the creatures or the army flooding the plain ahead of him. This man's attention was turned up toward the strange dim light that came from the sun.

Pierre watched as this chieftain raised his massive, muscular arms to the sky. Perfectly balanced despite the chariot's bumpy ride down the glacier, this man was poised and steady. His arms rose and fell, and though Pierre could not hear him, the sorcerer-chief was shouting out something, a spell of some kind, toward the sky.

The Frenchman looked upward and was shocked. The sun faded and then reversed its colors, shrinking back in upon itself so that only a golden rim, a perfect shining ring, surrounded the newly formed black disk in the sky. That dimness, the haze through which Pierre saw the world, only intensified. It was as if the world had gone inside-out.

Suddenly, time seemed to slow down, to nearly pause completely. For a brief second or two, everything in the world was suspended, only moving in a kind of super-slow motion. The men below didn't seem to notice; they were only concentrating on their race into battle.

And then, a horrific and repulsive detonation issued from the sky high above, its shockwave rolling through the air and pummeling every surface of the land below. The grasses rippled in waves, leaves and branches flew from the trees, and loose snow blew up from the glacier. This shockwave, and its accompanying explosion of darkness, showered the army below. In unison, the warriors stumbled slightly as the energy passed, and then they caught their balance and continued their forward progress.

Pierre thought the heavens had erupted and the end of the world was at hand. Indeed, it sounded as if the entire world was nearly rent in two. Looking up, he saw the black of the sun expanded in the sky, doubling its previous size. The once beautiful herald of life had become a frightful and malevolent force.

Banking downward again, the Frenchman's attention was caught by the wolf-clad army. As they ran, their bodies began to tremble and shake. Their heads snapped from side to side. Along their black painted skin, the jagged red patterns began to glow as if the men were burning up from within. Cords on their neck muscles strained as the warrior's jaws clenched tightly, their teeth visible between curled lips. The whites of their eyes disappeared behind ever-tightening lids, and the warriors' faces were completely hidden in black. Pierre could easily see the intense pain each man felt, but still each raced on across the plain, never breaking stride. On still each raced through the haze of darkness, that intensifying dim that enwrapped the world.

And then, unbelievably, the wolf fur each man wore began to creep its way down and along the warriors' bodies, enveloping each one in a black shroud. These cloaks, once flapping along in the breeze created by the army's passage, now fused tightly with the warrior's skins. Pierre watched, horrified, as the dark, unruly fur inched its way down the men's arms and legs, across their chests, and over their feet and hands, completely covering every bit of human skin.

The warriors' heads were twitching so fast they become a blur. The lines between man and beast crossed, then blended.

Once dead, the coal-black eyes in the wolves' heads now came alive, glowing in an evil golden light. The wolf jaws convulsed, sharp fangs thrusting out and forward.

The humans' white eyes and teeth disappeared as the warriors' black faces were swallowed up behind the newly reformed wolf visage.

A new creature emerged where each warrior had once been.

Pierre gasped, unblinking. He had seen one of these creatures before. He had seen it all too well and far too intimately. It continued to haunt his nightmares and thoughts, threatening to overpower the last remnants of his sanity. It attacked him on the earthen mound and it killed his companions and friends. Even now, while he slept, as this epic dream, this vision of the past, unfolded in his mind, the creature continued to track him in the real world.

By the darkest magic imaginable, conjured up from the evil powers of the sorcerer-chief, the wolf and the warrior had become one, completely inseparable.

Rushing forward across the plain, now at an even greater speed and ferocity, was an entire army of the *Nagual*, the skin-walkers, the Dogmen. These monsters, these demons, added their own aura of darkness to the world, like the heat that emanated from a glowing hot iron.

Once spellbound, Pierre finally looked away, unable to watch the transformations any longer. He gagged, his mind and stomach feeling as sick as the dim world around him.

His attention was soon caught by movement across the valley, opposite from the *Nagual*. It seemed as if the trees at the edge of the great forest were moving, coming forward, stepping out into the dim. And yet it wasn't trees that Pierre saw leaving the safety of the primeval forest.

A second army, once out of the tree cover, began to rush forward into the vast plain. Pierre wasn't quite close enough to see these new warriors in detail, but he could tell they were humanoid. But that wasn't quite accurate, either. This new army, apparently heading into battle against the *Nagual*, wasn't made up of humans. These creatures were far too big to be humans. Indeed, Pierre at first thought they were the trees because of their girth and height. In some ways, they resembled gigantic bears, but they were truly bipedal, moving with the grace and poise of men, and easily traversing on two legs.

But Pierre could clearly see that they were not human, instead they were huge, brutish beings, their bodies completely covered with long, draping hair. The colors of their fur ranged from a dark brown and russet to a speckled gray to lighter tones of tan and beige. The wiry strands of hair blocked out nearly every detail of the creatures' faces and hands. But the one detail the Frenchman could see very clearly was the beasts' oversized, bare feet. These appeared in all ways like human feet, only they were nearly comical due to their sheer size and width.

Most of these approaching creatures carried huge wooden clubs that swung in unison with their arms, pumping forward and back as they ran. They were a fierce, determined race, of that Pierre was sure. Judging by their numbers, however, they were surely outnumbered.

Pierre had no idea of the allegiance of this new army, but he did know one thing. If they were setting out to battle the Dogmen, they were clearly on the opposite side of pure evil.

An eternity passed as the two armies ran headlong toward each other across the vast plain. Strangely, Pierre could feel the rumble of their pounding footfalls on the hard-packed earth. That deep base not only echoed through the air, but also reverberated in his very bones. On one side, the army of *Nagual* was weaponless except for the razor sharp claws and jaws. Opposite the Dogmen, the hairy, manlike giants plodded on, their tree-trunk clubs moving rhythmically with the treading of their massive, unclad feet.

The gap between the armies suddenly closed, and the battle commenced. The front lines of the *Nagual* leapt high into the air, arms and legs spread wide. Some were beaten backward by the hairy giants' powerful club swings. Those Dogmen who dodged the blows landed nimbly upon the heads and shoulders of their enemies, biting and clawing and otherwise hanging on for dear life as huge hands reached upward, attempting to squeeze the life from their bodies.

A thunderous rumble resounded across the plain as the ranks of the two armies collided. Hundreds of skirmishes occurred up and down the battle line. Bones and throats were crushed in the iron grip of the giants. Keen-edged claws sank into flesh. Stout wooden clubs crunched skulls. Blood spurted, staining the ground below. But despite being vastly outnumbered, the hairy giants seemed to be getting the best of the *Nagual* army. Having seen the terrific might of one Dogman up close, Pierre could hardly imagine it being overpowered by any creature. But it was happening right here, before his very eyes.

And then the field was leveled. Blinding streaks of jagged lightning shot down from the heavens, one after another, striking the giants. The bolts that missed their targets bored huge craters in the tundra, sending fiery chunks of rock and soil in all directions. As the Frenchman watched, one giant was lit up, the charge so powerful that for a moment the beast's very skeleton glowed an eerie white all the way through its hairy skin. The club the giant carried burst into flames as the creature fell to its knees.

Soon, other spells cast by the sorcerer-chief blasted their way through the battlefield, knocking the *Nagual's* enemies down, making them much more vulnerable. The giants fought hard, but there was no telling how much longer they could last against the sheer numbers of the Dogmen.

The battle raged on as Pierre's vantage point again rose higher into the air. Looking back toward the direction from where the *Nagual* army had come, he saw more creatures rumbling their way down the foothills to join the fray. They were fantastical beasts that his brain could hardly fathom. Some of these were human-shaped, yet their bulging bodies were topped with thick, spiraling horns like those of a wild ram. Other creatures were even larger than those that pulled the sorcerer-chief's cart. They plowed ahead at a near sprint on four massive, tree-like legs, their fur in shaggy, long strings that blew back up behind them from the rush of air. But they were twice as tall at the shoulder, and instead of a long horn at the front of their heads there were not only a pair of tusks, each longer than a man, but also what appeared to be a muscular, hairy arm that swayed back and forth, announcing its coming. Clad in simple leather and bone armor, human-looking foot soldiers racing alongside were cautious to stay out of the path of these great beasts, though as Pierre watched, one man got too close, slipped, and was flattened into goo beneath the beast's heavy footfalls.

Atop these behemoths rode determined warriors, their bodies covered in some sort of spiked armor, clutching wicked-looking spears.

And still more and more monsters appeared all along the battlefront, and Pierre could stand it no longer, seeing the horrific combinations that composed each. He turned his view toward the far distant forest again to see reinforcements leaving the tree cover and coming to the aid of the hairy giants. These were far too far away for him to discern any details, but their numbers would help tremendously. He felt momentary relief that this army, the enemies of the *Nagual*, might still stand a chance. There was no sense of loyalty to these giants. *But the enemy of my enemy is bound to be my friend*, he thought.

But he'd had enough. The battle, the fantastic and awful creatures, all of it was just too much. Pierre was truly overjoyed as his flight turned and headed back toward the spot from where he'd first began this dream journey. The haze of darkness was already being mingled with the dust of the battle below. The world was becoming dimmer all around him. The Frenchman had no desire to look back or see any more of the chaos.

Thank God this dream is finally ending, he thought, allowing it to echo through his mind.

The details of the world faded with the diminishing of the light, and Pierre could feel himself exhale in relief that this vision was only just that—a dream.

But suddenly he was hit in mid-air, and the dream world regained focus. He somersaulted, the sky tumbling atop the land over and over as one replaced the other. Gray, blue, green, beige, a muted kaleidoscope exploded in front of his eyes. And the impact hurt! He distinctly felt pain in his neck, back, and legs. *That can't be*, he thought. *You can't feel pain in a dream.*

Finally regaining a semblance of balance, he realized he was dizzy. *How can I feel dizzy in a dream?* he thought. Now he was confused. If this was a dream, how could he feel sensations so real? *Unless maybe...what if this wasn't just a dream?*

His vision cleared and he found himself diving downward at full speed. The ground rushed up to meet him. Everything around him became a blur. His heart seemed to be crawling right up through his throat. His chest tightened up. For two long seconds, Pierre thought for sure that he was going to die—he would surely smash upon the rocky ground below.

Right at the last second, however, he pulled up just a few feet above the ground and gracefully arced, banking sharply to the left, then back to the right. His view was still manipulated – someone or something else was in control, and he was only watching through its eyes. It was during this second change of direction that the Frenchman got a look behind him and saw what made these evasive maneuvers so vital. There was some sort of creature chasing him! A momentary glance was more than enough, as the details burned into his memory.

Like everything else in this world, his pursuer was gigantic. Pierre's mind couldn't fathom something of that size having the ability to fly. It was a shiny black in color, and Pierre thought it was covered in a slick, flattened fur, but it could just as easily been tightly packed feathers. However, those weren't the details that really caught his eye.

The flying beast resembled a wolverine, a long, slinking wild cat, or another sort of normal north woods animal with which Pierre was already familiar. However, this beast was easily the same size as the horned creatures that pulled the sorcerer-chief's war chariot below. Keeping it aloft were long, leathery wings like those of a bat, each of them two or three times the length of its body, that continuously beat the air.

Despite its size, it seemed very agile, and it had no problem countering the maneuvers Pierre's dream vehicle could make.

The Frenchman got another peek as he banked and turned in a dizzying combination of maneuvers. The pursuing creature's head seemed far too big for its body. Its snout was pushed in like that of a wild cat, but its wide mouth, slightly open, revealed rows of long, razor-sharp teeth. *That thing could easily swallow a man*, he thought grimly. *No biting, no chewing, just gone. And is that thing smiling at me?*

Ahead of the creature, its long front arms reached out with deadly clawed fingers. And Pierre thought he saw a long, snaky tail stretching out behind the monster. Of course, the worst was its eyes. They glowed an evil yellow just like the Dogmen below.

Turn led into turn, but still the monster kept pace. Pierre began to feel tired, completely exhausted. Again, he had no idea how he could be feeling sensations in a dream, but here they were nonetheless. Despite the quick banking and careening through the air, he was sure the monster was gaining on him.

Was it his imagination, this dream-turned-nightmare, creating the stench of the pursuing creature's putrid breath that filled the air all around him? Was it his imagination making the hairs stand up straight on his neck in mortal fear? Was it his imagination that made his heart pound in his chest and his lungs ache to be filled with air?

Suddenly, a sharp blow pierced his lower extremities and Pierre screamed, pain exploding all over his body. It was no ordinary wound; it felt like he was both on fire and also that his veins were freezing from the inside out. Whatever aberrant abilities this creature possessed, its vicious attack was supernatural at the very least. Pierre was sure that he had been poisoned, and that this infection was already eating away at his insides. Whatever venom had been passed into his system was seizing and knotting his muscles, and the pain was excruciating.

Within moments, Pierre's forward movement ceased, and he began falling again, plummeting toward the ground like a dropped stone. This time, he knew there was no pulling out of that dive. His dead weight dragged him faster and faster toward the earth, and the ground rushed up to meet him. He screamed again, his voice lost in the blast of wind as the world blurred around him.

***

Still screaming, Pierre awoke to the darkness of the predawn forest. His chest was heaving as he struggled to catch his breath. Sweat yet again poured down his face despite the cold of the night around him. The little bit of blue-violet light from the sky created silhouettes from the thin trees all around his camp. These shapes swam in his dizzying vision, both confusing and terrifying him.

Pierre realized the silence of the forest as soon as his screams echoed into nothingness. His mouth kept working on the scream though no more sounds issued forth. And then reality sank back to him. He wasn't dead. He wasn't dying. He wasn't prey to some bizarre creature.

He was here, back in the *Michigana* country, tucked into a tightly grown copse of trees and shrubbery with a few large pines sheltering him from the worst of the wind. The snow was still pushed up into walls around his sleeping nook.

His little fire had burned down to gray ashes that blew up in spiraling circles from the light breeze that was sneaking into his abode. His eyes locked onto the couple of emerging, glowing red coals until he could steady himself. The warm coals were comforting, easing his shock and pushing the remnants of his nightmare far back into the recesses of his mind.

Slowly, his breath returned and his heart stopped racing. He tried to take a lungful of the cold *Michigana* air, but coughed it back out immediately. *Too much too quickly*, he told himself. The next smaller breaths came more easily. Pierre put his hands up to his face and rubbed the rough skin, the long hair and beard, the tired eyes that had seen so much in the dream world.

Dream world, or real world? Imagined or real? Or was there really any line between them anymore? Again, he thought that he was losing his mind. He was afraid that his mind was slowly leaving him at any rate. He pushed his hands up to his forehead and ran his fingers slowly through the long hair on his scalp. The dizziness left him, but something else had taken its place. Trepidation? Apprehension? No, it felt like much more than that. It was as if there was something missing from his mind, something important taken out. And yet that hole in his mind had been filled back up with an intense fear bubbling up just below the surface, always ready to boil over and scald him with terrifying panic and dread.

Again, the warmth of the coals pulled him back, back from the trap his mind had become. He concentrated on the comforting glow as his hands automatically spread themselves over the fire, seeking the little heat that remained.

Pierre allowed himself one peek into the memory of his nightmare. *The Nagual I recognized,* he thought to himself. *But I had no idea there could be so many of them. Just one in this world was more than enough. And what were those other beasts and monsters?* He'd never heard of, never even imagined, any such animals that resembled what he saw in his nightmare.

Of course, with the horror of this latest nightmare only just receding, this line of thinking led to only one very important question. *If the Dogman could cross into our world, what might keep those other beasts from doing the same?*

There was no answer, not from the wind high in the barren tree branches, not from the lonely hoot of an owl in the far distance, not from the sky that was quickly lightening from violet to indigo.

The Frenchman could only force himself to go on. His mind might be deteriorating, poisoned with the horrific and incomprehensible images of ages and cultures long past, but his instincts for survival here in the present would not permit him to stop. The fort at Mackinac was still a long way off, but it was closer with each step he took.

Physically, Pierre was revived and prepared for this journey. But his nightmares would eventually consume him, completely obliterating his sanity before he reached his destination.

BOOK 2
August 1977

CHAPTER 1
Arrival

The last bright fingers of sunlight slipped through the tree trunks. Total darkness wouldn't occur for another hour or more, but the night was making itself at home. Not that the darkness brought any relief from the heat. August evenings in northern Michigan are still hot even though each day continues to shrink a few minutes shorter.

The second week of August brought with it the dog days of summer.

In the tourist towns and resorts, in cabins and cottages, the summer folk were already thinking about returning south. Boats would soon be dry docked and then cleaned up at the local marinas. Last projects, delayed with the hustle and bustle of get-togethers, were finally finished up, whether it be painting the shutters, staining the deck, or putting the storms back in the upstairs windows. Kids became increasingly restless, dreading the return to school in only a few weeks.

Still the business of summer continued. There were still picnics, camp fires, dinner parties, and the occasional firework display. There were still a couple of festivals and art fairs. But for those who weren't permanent residents, August represented the time to wind down. Phone calls were made to the plumbers, contractors, and the occasional handyman, setting dates for winterizing the homes, taking out the docks, draining the pipes, and changing over the phone and mail service. Lawns were going to be cut for the last time before the mowers were stashed in the garage.

Weekends were still hectic as the weekend warriors invaded, making their escape from their busy everyday lives (and yet bringing the bustle of the cities up north with them). But during the week, most towns and villages in northern Michigan were rather quiet and peaceful as folks went about their day-to-day responsibilities.

***

In Benzie County's Platte River State Forest, a bit west of Traverse City, two young men were just finishing up dinner. Dan Greene, the chef extraordinaire, had whipped up a smorgasbord of dehydrated chicken soup, freeze-dried lasagna, and chocolate pudding for dessert. It was an easy dinner— just add the right amount of water boiled from Dan's little camping stove. Backpacking, especially for long treks, called for lightweight, easily prepared meals, as they had to be hauled in and the garbage had to be hauled out.

Hiking up to 15 miles each day and carrying 60 pounds on their backs burned a lot of calories, and the two men needed to constantly replenish their spent energy. In fact, for a trip of this magnitude, foodstuffs took up the bulk of the space in their packs.

Dan's best friend, Bryan King, was lazily leaning against an old oak, his fingers locked behind his head. Both feet were propped up on his backpack. Bryan was in full relax mode now, the weariness of the day's hike draining away.

"Don't forget to put up the bear bag after dinner," Dan called to his friend. "I don't know what made those tracks we found today, but whatever it is, it's big."

"And probably not too friendly," added Bryan, pulling a granola bar out of the side pocket of his backpack. "Did you see the points of the claws at the end? They were dug in deeper than the track itself."

"You got any idea what it was?" Dan asked from across their camp. The clearing they chose this evening was roughly a hundred feet across, though most of it was still covered by the long, crooked branches of the oaks and pines all around. As always, they pitched their little tent on high ground, though there wasn't much chance of rain. It was just a good habit to have when camping.

"No clue," responded Bryan, who was munching on his snack. "Could have been a wolf or a bear maybe. Might even be a cougar. I hear they've got 'em around here. The only tracks I really know are deer."

"Last thing we need is some critter ripping up our food bag," said Dan. "I mean, what do you think, are we still about two days out of Benzonia? Pretty good distance to go without eating if something gets our food."

"Might even be three days at your speed," joked Bryan, checking his trail map now that his granola bar was gone. "If something were to happen, and I'm just saying *if*, we'd probably do better heading for this little village called Honor. It doesn't look very big on the map, but it probably has a store or something."

A minute went by as Bryan studied the map and Dan drew designs in the dirt with his hiking stick. Both were lost in their thoughts; both were thinking about large, dangerous carnivores.

"I don't think cat tracks show the claw imprints," Dan said slowly. "I'm pretty sure they retract 'em when they walk.

But you're right on about it not being friendly. Claws that big are made for one thing—killing prey."

A little nervously, Bryan answered, "It's not our food I'm concerned about. An animal with claws that big might be more interested in us than in our food. We don't have anything to defend ourselves, and last time I checked, you can't outrun a bear."

"I don't have to outrun a bear," joked Dan, smiling slyly. He threw an acorn across the campsite where it bounced off of Bryan's boot. "I just got to outrun you, pal."

The two had been roommates the past two years at Northern Michigan University. They both loved being in the outdoors, and had taken many weekend trips backpacking all around the Upper Peninsula. This summer, they'd both taken off the last three weeks of work for a much greater challenge. Their goal was to backpack 100 miles along the West Michigan Scenic Trail from Kalkaska to Manistee, to the home of their other roommate, Jim, who would be returning from his internship in Germany by the time they got there. Otherwise, he would have been on the trip with them.

They were only a little more than halfway through the hike. No one would be expecting them for more than a week.

"I'm gonna take the dishes down to that little stream we passed before it gets too dark," Bryan said, pushing himself up. Since Dan cooked, it was Bryan's job to clean up.

"Bring back a jug of water, too," Dan said, tipping their collapsible plastic jug upside down. A few drops fell to the pine needles on the forest floor. "As you can see, we're out."

Rummaging in his pack, Bryan pulled out the bear bag and the length of rope. "Why don't you hang the food while I'm down there?"

But Dan was already on his feet heading off to the woods. "Sorry, man, can't do. When nature calls, you gotta answer."

Gathering up the cooking pot, the bowls and silverware, and a Brillo pad together in a mesh bag, Bryan slipped a finger through the handle of the water jug and walked off toward the stream. It was a couple of hundred feet back the way they'd come and then down a little ravine. His hiking boots only slipped a little on the stones and loose dirt, but he'd have to be careful on the way back up, especially since it was getting dark. Large ferns brushed his legs.

The little stream was only a few inches deep and maybe 10 feet across. The clear water swirled around the rocks and logs in the river bed. But it was just right for whipping up the dishes. Bryan worked quickly, swatting away the mosquitoes that were swarming all around him.

And then, a horrific, agonizing scream split the otherwise silent woods. Bryan straightened up, eyes wide open. That enormous clawed track was the only thing registering in his mind. Whatever made that track had obviously attacked his friend. He dropped his cooking pot on the stream bank and sprinted back to camp, leaving everything behind.

Adrenaline pumped through his system as he scrambled up the ravine and then ran full speed along the path. Dan liked to joke and have fun, but that scream was nothing to laugh about. Bryan's heart was racing, partly in fear about what might have happened to his friend and also for what danger he might be heading into himself.

As soon as Bryan reached their camp clearing, he saw the animal. It appeared to be a wolf, but it was huge! Granted, he'd never seen a wolf in the wild, but this one dwarfed the wolves he'd seen at the Detroit Zoo as a kid. *Maybe they grow this big in the wild*, he thought. It must have been four feet tall at the shoulder. *God, it's the size of a bear!*

Dan was nowhere to be seen.

Pushing back his fear, Bryan puffed out his chest and tried to act intimidating. He'd heard that someplace, that wild animals are more afraid of humans than humans are of them. If you made a lot of noise, you could scare them away. Bryan raised his arms up over his head, hands and fingers curved in a threatening posture, and yelled, "Go away!"

But the wolf only looked at him, its yellow eyes glowing in the near darkness. Though impossible to tell in the twilight, it looked as if there was blood covering the wolf's muzzle.

Then, to Bryan's surprise, the wolf stood upright, raised its own front paws to head level, and growled loudly back at him.

Bryan's jaw dropped at the same time his arms fell back to his side. *Not good*, he thought. *Not good at all.*

The creature (at this point he was pretty sure it was not a wolf) took a threatening step forward, and Bryan knew he was in trouble. Deep trouble.

He shot quick glances all around the clearing and saw the one tree that would work. It was only a couple of strides away, and it might be his only chance. Bryan judged the lowest branch to be about 10 feet up, but if he got a running start...

The wolf snarled and dropped back to all fours. It continued to stare at him, almost daring him to make the first move.

One shot at this, Bryan thought.

His body tensed as he prepared to make his move. It would be close, but he thought he could outrun the creature. Once he got up into the branches he should be okay.

The wolf pounded its two front paws on the ground, and spooked by it, Bryan took off.

Two more steps with his long legs and he'd reached the tree. In one fluid movement, he planted his left foot solidly on the tree trunk and kicked off with all of his might. His body propelled upward and his arms reached for the branch. For the briefest of moments, suspended in mid-air, he thought he'd miscalculated it. He was sure his fingers would come up just short.

He was a natural tree climber and had been since he was a child. It was easy, despite his panic, to shimmy up the branches.

Bryan perched himself on what appeared to be the last stout limb, about 20 feet up. And even this one was bowed with his weight. Those branches above him were much smaller in diameter and he didn't want to try going any higher. Besides, he thought, I should be safe at this height.

Looking down and catching his breath, Bryan watched as the huge wolf slowly circled his tree.

I can wait it out, he thought. *I can stay up here all night.*

And then, to Bryan's horror, the creature began climbing the tree. It didn't hurry. It didn't jump for the first branch like the human did, though it could have easily without a running start. In fact, it didn't use any branches at all. It simply sunk its claws into the trunk and steadily pulled its way upward.

The creature looked up at Bryan the entire way. And it was grinning at him in a most evil and unnatural manner. It was as if the creature were savoring the moment, enjoying the fear it provoked in the human trapped above. Bryan took one last look down at the creature. *That is blood on its muzzle*, he thought.

Bryan attempted to make it one more branch up, but it simply bent under his weight and his feet landed back where he'd been.

There was nowhere to go.

***

It first happened at 1:37 a.m.

Folks all over the area had been tucked away in bed, most having been asleep for several hours already.

The Boar's Head Roadhouse had closed up at 11, the last pair of well-wishers sent out into the northern Michigan night to seek their fortunes. As Tina the bartender always said at that time of night, "You don't have to go home, but you can't stay here."

It was heard across the fields and orchards of western Grand Traverse County. It rolled across the hills and valleys of eastern Benzie County. It echoed through the dense forests and swept across the still lake waters.

It was a lonely and deserted cry.

But it was also so much more.

The awful, blood-curdling howl reverberated through homes, chilling the inhabitants right to the bone.

Within a few seconds, lights popped on in half the houses in the area, their windows creating little fishbowls inside their homes. The other half stayed dark as the owners huddled together, too frozen in fear to leave the relative safety of their beds.

Dogs for miles around began a chorus of barking, though even they were glad it was only heard from a distance. No self-respecting dog would want to meet the owner of that howl.

Horses and livestock stirred uneasily in their pens and barns before tightly packing themselves against each other for safety. The warm afternoon sun would be shining before they once again dispersed themselves and actually began eating.

Every other animal within earshot of that awful howl tucked itself down and hid in the most remote place that it could find.

Old Charlie Cooper, Lake Ann's local handyman and caretaker, actually did jump right out of bed. He landed on the worn carpet of his little two-room cabin, looking in all directions even though he couldn't see a thing in the darkness. A bead of sweat had appeared on his wrinkly forehead, and he was breathing so rapidly that a few moments later he thought that maybe he was having a heart attack.

***

The seven bunkhouses were in a state of chaos at Camp Doubennet. The residents, all between the ages of 9 and 15, were in varying degrees of panic. The counselors, not much older themselves, had an awful time attempting to regain order.

Camp Director Ted "Champ" Champlain, the old man who owned and ran the camp, made the rounds to each bunkhouse trying his best to calm and reassure the kids.

The counselors in the Woodchuck, Raccoon, Porcupine, and Wolf cabins did everything they could think of to distract the kids by playing games, singing old camp songs, and telling stories.

The Bear and Cougar cabins with the oldest kids were only a little bit better. The counselors had every camper drag his mattress pad to the floor in the middle of each building where they made one gigantic bed.

Even the 15-year-olds, generally the kids who thought of themselves as "too cool" or "too old" for many of the typical camp activities, were frightened. Not their usual, talkative selves, they remained silent now. Harried eyes darted constantly to the windows and doors. Any creak in the old cabin brought whimpers and cries from the kids.

Of course, the Chipmunk Cabin was particularly chaotic, because it was where the youngest campers stayed. These nine-year-olds, aptly named the "Chipmunks" of the camp, generally had the most difficulty adjusting to life away from their parents. They were often homesick, and undoubtedly two or three normally would head home early from camp.

Chris Young, the nearly 18-year-old head counselor of the Chipmunk Cabin, was spooked himself. But he knew he had to stay calm. If he reacted in a panic, he and the other counselors would lose total control of the situation. First, of course, he had flicked on the overhead lights. The couple of bare light bulbs along the cabin's peak weren't great, but they were better than nothing. Then he had surveyed the situation and tried to develop a plan.

Known for his level-headedness and maturity, Chris had been working at Camp Doubennet for four years. Though he was younger than some of the other counselors, including his own assistant, he had more experience than anybody currently working there (except for Champ). Once a camper himself, Chris loved the camp and Champ, who was like a father to him, so much that he had wanted to work there in the summers. In that time, he'd really become Champ's right-hand man, knowing nearly every detail about running the camp.

A group of four little boys were huddled together on the lower bunk in one corner of the cabin. They would have looked rather comical under any other circumstances, their arms hugging each other and their bed sheets pulled up to their necks.

Jack Schoenveld, a junior counselor and Chris's assistant, had his arm around one little boy who was standing in the middle of the room, sobbing uncontrollably, his pillow clutched in a death grip against his chest. Despite his best efforts, Jack couldn't get the young camper to calm down.

Chris was on his way to help Jack when the cabin door creaked open. Every kid shrieked in unison. But they piped down a moment later when Champ walked in, holding his lantern.

Chris pulled the older man aside. In a low voice he said, "Hey Champ, I'm glad you're here, man. We need help. The kids are goin' nuts and we can't get 'em settled down."

"The Woodchuck Cabin's not much better," responded the camp director grimly, looking over the situation. He ran the fingers of his free hand through his thin, gray hair. "I think we ought to take your kids and theirs over to the mess hall. Strength in numbers and all that, you know. They'll feel better when there's more of 'em together."

He gave Chris a half smile. This young man was his right-hand man, the one counselor at the camp who had Champ's total confidence. Despite the chaotic circumstances, Champ was very proud of Chris's leadership on display this very moment. "Besides, we can get out a few tubs of ice cream. I don't know any kid who didn't feel better after a sundae."

"This would have to happen the last week of camp, wouldn't it?" Chris said with a sigh.

Champ gave a snort. "Yeah, I don't know if we can handle four more days of this."

They both looked around the room. Jack now had a throng assembled around him. But most of the cabin's 20 campers were still spread around the room in pairs or threes babbling nervously. No one was anywhere near a window.

"I'll bet it's probably just a bear or wolf or something just passin' through," Chris said, running his fingers through his shoulder-length blond hair, just as his mentor had done a few moments earlier. "But it won't help our retention rate. There'll be a few of these kids who won't be back next summer."

The camp needed its residents to come back year after year. Most of their advertising was done by word of mouth with happy kids and parents selling the camp to their friends downstate. But numbers had been decreasing over the past few years, and Champ was always worried about the retention rates, since those were the kids that filled up most of the camp roster.

Champ could have put Chris in charge of any group in the camp, including the oldest Bears. But the director knew his best man should be with the youngest campers. Chris always gave the kids the best experience and hooked them for the next couple of years.

"Can't worry 'bout that now," Champ said, the sound of resignation in his voice. "Let's take care of tonight. Maybe we can salvage some of it." He gave Chris a knowing wink, and the young counselor smiled back. If there was anybody on the staff who could salvage an evening as rough as this one, it would be Chris.

Holding the screen door open, Champ said, "I'll lead us over. You all just follow the light."

Chris moved to the center of the cabin. Blowing once on his whistle, Chris turned all eyes on himself. "Okay everybody, I want you all to grab your pillow and flashlight and meet me in the middle of the room. Right now." He blew the whistle a second time and the kids sprang into action.

The Chipmunks were tightly clustered around their taller counselor in only a few seconds. Little circles of light from their flashlights wiggled all over the floor. Their big, watery eyes looked up, waiting for direction. They all admired and respected Chris, who was their leader, the big brother of the cabin.

"Let's all grab hands and make a line," Chris said calmly to the kids. "Jack, you take the back end, and I'll lead the front."

As soon as the kids were all linked, Chris looked down at them and smiled warmly. "Okay, now I know you're all scared. It's okay to feel that way. But I want you to know you're safe with me and Jack. Here's what we're gonna do. We're gonna walk over to the mess hall and Champ's got some ice cream for us."

He could see apprehension on the kids' faces, though a few lit up at the mention of ice cream. But none of them wanted to go out in the dark. "You've got to trust us—nothing's gonna happen to you. You're safe with me and Jack." Chris nodded to his assistant, and Jack nodded back.

"Now, is everybody linked up?" asked Chris. Twenty little heads nodded. "Good. Hold hands all the way. We're gonna go at a fast walk, but nobody runs. Okay?" Again, the campers nodded.

It might only have been 50 yards to the mess hall, but it felt like a mile. The crescent moon had fallen a few hours earlier and it was very dark outside. Of course, millions of stars were visible since there were no cities nearby to provide light pollution. The kids weren't interested in the stars, however; they were just concentrating on getting into the mess hall quickly and safely.

Seen from a distance, the long line of flashlights in the darkness resembled a glowing caterpillar. Most of the lights bounced along the ground, though a few occasionally shined up on the trees and shrubbery. At the head of the line, Champ's lantern illuminated a circle perhaps 10 feet across.

Having walked this path hundreds of times, Chris was very familiar with every rock and root along the way. But tonight, it all felt strange, like a dark, alien landscape. He even lost track of where they were. Champ had not been to the mess hall yet, so there were no lights on in the building to guide the campers.

Tonight, everything seemed out of place. That awful howling every few minutes changed everything, casting a creepy sense over everything. The night was still and quiet. Usually there was a cacophony of frog chirps and insect buzzing.

And then, seemingly from everywhere around them, that same horrific growl echoed through the camp. The nice, straight line of lights instantly went berserk. Little beams of light flashed in all directions, and a couple of flashlights hit the ground as frightened fingers spastically opened. The kids squealed and screamed.

"Grab hands!" yelled Chris. "Grab hands right now!"

The screaming died to whimpering and the group tightened up in a mass. Champ's lantern shined up over the group. "Is everyone okay? Are you all here?" he asked.

Tear-streaked faces nodded up at the camp director. The kids' eyes were wide and filled with fright.

"Then let's get going again. We're almost there," Champ said calmly. "I know you're scared but everything's gonna be fine."

Somewhere in the distance, a twig snapped. Everyone jumped. Flashlights shined in all directions.

"Let's go," Chris said forcefully. "Now!"

This time, the campers moved as a whole group. The going was a bit slower as they tried not to stumble over each other. Dark shadows filled in the empty space between the tree trunks, the tall ferns, and the underbrush that their flashlights illuminated on the side of the path.

Time seemed to slow to a crawl. Though they felt the rush to reach their destination, every step took an eternity. The kids gasped at every noise, every slight rustle in the woods around them. And there was no judging distance in the blackness of the night.

Finally, Champ's lantern picked up the chipped concrete patio outside the mess hall's main door. Two seconds later, Champ was opening the screen door and then the hall's heavy main door.

The camp director stepped inside and flicked the light switch. He was instantly mobbed by the campers who piled their way into the mess hall, pillows and flashlights tumbling in all directions. Half of the kids began running around the tables, burning off the adrenaline and energy that had built up in their system. The rest stayed huddled in a group near the serving window that led to the kitchen.

Exhaling deeply, Champ set the lantern down on the countertop next to the door and walked into the kitchen. His goal was to get these kids set up quickly with a nice treat and then head back for the campers in the Woodchuck Cabin.

Chris started gathering the campers who were milling about either fretting or in a daze. But he whipped around when he heard Jack's panicking voice cut through the expanse of the dining hall.

"I only count 19," Jack said, already frantically recounting the kids. He wasn't one to think or act well under pressure, and he was only creating more panic among the campers. His index fingers were moving through the air like a crazed music conductor.

In a commanding tone, Chris said, "Everybody sit down. Now." The kids immediately dropped to the floor wherever in the lodge they were. When they were situated and as still as could be expected, Chris spoke again. "Look around. Who's missing?"

The kids all leaned over and looked around at each other. Their eyes were searching for their friends' faces in the crowd.

"Nolan!" cried one little boy. "Where's Nolan?"

Suddenly, everyone was frantically looking all around the mess hall. But they all knew that little Nolan was missing. He was easily overlooked, being the smallest boy in camp. Nolan was even tiny compared to the other boys in his cabin. And he was one of the quietest, never drawing attention to himself.

"Champ, we need you!" Jack hollered through the open serving area into the camp kitchen.

But Chris was already sprinting for the door. "No, I'll go. You guys keep the other kids busy. Get 'em their ice cream." He paused just long enough to grab Champ's lantern from the table by the entrance.

The screen door shut with a slam as Chris bounded off into the darkness. Even with Champ's lantern, there was very little to see. Chris scowled. The lantern wasn't much help; it only cast a little bit of light a few feet on all sides.

It was as if the camp Chris always loved had been swept away into the black hole that this night had become.

Keep your head, he told himself. *We came down the path from the cabin. Just follow it back.*

"Nolan!" Chris cried into the night, oblivious to whatever else might be within earshot. "Nolan! It's me, Chris. Where are you?"

But the only answer was the buzzing of the mosquitoes around his ears. Annoyed, he shooed them away and pushed on down the path.

He kept yelling into the darkness. "Nolan! I'm here to get you, buddy! Just let me know where you are!"

Suddenly, Chris stumbled. His arms and hands went out wide to regain his balance. Looking down, he saw the dirty pillow he'd tripped over.

"Nolan!" he yelled again. "I know you're right around here. Let me know where you are and I'll get you to the mess hall."

Shining Champ's lantern in a widening circle, Chris finally saw a bright spot in the darkness, tucked between a trio of wide oak trees. A little white face peered back at him, dark eyes reflecting back in the lantern's beam.

Kneeling down, Chris put his arms around the little boy. "I'm so glad you're okay."

Nolan was sobbing, silently. "I...I...I was s-so s-s-scared. I counna move."

"It's okay, kid," Chris said soothingly. "I'm gonna take you to the mess hall. You're safe now."

And then something appeared in the lantern light over Chris's shoulder.

Nolan shrieked and Chris whirled around, his ears ringing and his face white with fear.

"God!" he screamed. "Champ, you scared the crap out of me!"

"Sorry," the camp director said abashed, his head dropping a little. "I didn't mean to scare you. Go ahead and take him to the mess hall. I'm gonna go get the Woodchucks." He raised his eyebrows as he tucked his lips around his teeth and sighed. "They're probably in the same boat."

Nolan slipped his little hand into Chris's. The counselor looked down at the little boy, then scooped him up in his arms and carried him down to the mess hall. Chris's muscles strained after a few dozen yards since the little kid was heavier than he looked. But the counselor's strength held out. Nolan didn't unlatch his arms from around Chris's neck until they were well within the lighted building and among the other campers who were already forgetting the night's scare with bowls of ice cream.

Around camp, most of the kids finally dozed off, mentally exhausted. But many didn't get back to sleep all night. And even though there were only a few days left before the camp closed for the summer, a couple of kids from each cabin did call home to be picked up early.

***

In downtown Interlochen, most students at the Green Lake Music Camp barely heard the howling, if they heard it at all. Since the dorms had no air conditioning, most students had old, rusty box fans in their window to keep the oppressive heat at bay. The few unlucky ones who had no means of beating the heat did hear the howl off in the distance, and these students hunkered down in fear beneath their covers despite the temperature.

***

Natalie Robbins was one of the few who was not immediately spooked by the howl, though her dog, Winnebago, was. Of course, "Winnie" was spooked by just about everything. It hardly seemed right for a huge Yellow Lab to be afraid of her own shadow. Natalie might not have been alarmed by the howl in the distance, but Winnie was terrified. The retriever circled the braided rug on Natalie's bedroom floor, her tail between her legs, whimpering the entire time.

Natalie, or "The Cherry Lady" as everyone knew her, sat up in bed and listened carefully to the night sounds outside the window screen. A light breeze rippled the leaves on the aspen and poplar trees in the back yard. Normally there would be a whole cacophony of sounds here in the remote regions of Grand Traverse County. But tonight, all was silent except for the wind through the leaves. *Not a creature was stirring*, she thought, the appropriate line from her favorite Christmas book coming to mind. *Except one. One creature's stirring up something big out there, I think.*

The howl came on again, and this time Natalie did shiver, despite the warmth of the early August night. In response, Winnie gave her own weak, warbling and pathetic howl that wouldn't be heard much past the back yard.

Though she'd never heard such a noise in her life—and she'd grown up in the greater Traverse City area and lived way out here in Lake Ann for many years—Natalie instinctively knew what it belonged to. The more she thought about it, the more certain she became. Her distant past, well over 50 years in the making, blasted its way back into the present as she recalled the old tribal legends her grandmother had told her when she was a little girl.

Of course, her Nana's versions of the beginnings of human civilization were rather at odds with the version taught in school. That was probably why Natalie had received such poor grades in social studies and history when she was little; what she learned at school just didn't match up with what she was taught at home.

Natalie frowned, curling her lips in against her teeth. She really didn't need any of this right now. It was bad enough that what little sleep she got these days was troubled by her business. Now she had wild critters interrupting her sleep and panicking her dog. "Come on up, girl," she said to Winnie. The dog was on the bed in a second, her nose immediately tucked under a fold of blanket. Winnie whimpered a few more times until Natalie stroked her neck and scratched behind her ears.

"It's okay, old girl. Everything's okay."

But Natalie had to wonder if everything was really okay. She'd thought back to some of the stories that had popped up around Manistee and Bear Lake this spring, and from Wexford County and further south many years ago. Normally she would have dismissed such stories as fantasy. The supposed "witnesses" would have been also brushed aside, called crackpots, probably drunk or under the influence of some drug or other.

Yet she'd grown up believing in the legends she'd heard from her Nana, even when world history and U.S. history and the study of civilizations drilled the common knowledge of human culture into her head. And these stories 10 or 20 years ago fit far too easily into the world her Nana had described to her. Nana's story world was a place of monsters and magic and heroes who stood against evil. And of course, the people of Nana's tribe were among the heroes who saved the world.

The howl in the distance didn't scare Natalie, but it did worry her. And at 58 years old, she didn't need more things to worry about at this point in her life.

For that cry had not been heard in that part of northern Michigan for thousands of years. The last time it occurred, the Great Lakes region was blanketed by a hundred feet of glacial ice.

CHAPTER 2
Encounters

The light fog was just lifting as the very rim of the sun peered above the treetops to the east. The early morning haze wasn't a good sign; it was sure to be another blazing hot day.

But for the moment, the grass was still wet with dew. Far across the pasture, a woodpecker drilled away, *rap-rap-rap*. It was a lonely sound, the only noise here to be heard in the farm country of western Benzie County. The world was completely still. No breeze to blow away the fog meant there was no breeze to animate the leaves.

"Well, *Doc*, what's yer take on it?" asked Deputy Jim Dorcy wearily. He still couldn't believe his bad luck to be on this particular call.

The small man looked up through his round spectacles. His eyes were magnified behind the lenses, giving him a silly, cartoonish appearance.

"Caaaan't say for cerrrtin," the veterinarian drawled out in an accent almost Southern. The little man's bald head and slow speech made him seem much older than his 31 years. Originally from southern Indiana, Doctor Stephen Steinebeck had moved to Benzonia in the fall of 1975 and had been practicing veterinary medicine in Benzie County ever since. It might not have been a heavily populated county, but there were plenty of farms and ranches that kept him hopping along.

"How long's it been dead, you think?" the deputy asked, spitting a squirt of brown juice on the ground off to the side of the potential crime scene. His lip was puffed out, a wad of chew tucked nicely in between it and his teeth.

"Wellll, you know I can't say for cerrrrtin..." the vet drawled on, his face wrinkled up in disgust at the lawman's bad habit.

The deputy sighed loudly. He had little use for the young veterinarian and his pokiness. Or for the social commentary that was plainly written across his face. "Yeah, we've been through this already. Give me your best guess, *Doc*."

The vet returned his attention to the dead animal he'd been hunkered beside. He reached out and brushed the horse's black mane with his gloved hand. The hair was stiff and it sprung back to its former position. "Then I'd haaave ta say 'bout two days, now. You can see the body's in full rigor." And then pointing, he said, "And you can see the larvae just appearin' here round the eyes and ears. Of course, we could have the crime lab confirm my best guess if you a-wants it, *deputy*." He emphasized the last word just as the lawman had emphasized 'Doc' earlier. It wasn't necessarily a sign of respect.

Deputy Dorcy scribbled a few lines in his little notebook, glaring at the vet over the top rims of his glasses. A few seconds later, his attention turned to the farmer who looked back indignantly.

"So how come you haven't known 'till now that this here animal's been missin' or dead?" the deputy asked, peering intently at the old man. If there was a crime here, it would be that Deputy Dorcy's morning was being wasted on this nonsense. It might be a simple case of neglect, which was a crime whether the animal was a pet or a farm animal. Nice open and shut case, probably wouldn't even need to be reported.

Budgets were tight and the prosecutor had much better things to do than go after the poor farmers at the edge of the county. A case of animal neglect wasn't exactly a glamorous crime to prosecute.

"I'll have you know I take good care of my animals, good care of 'em. 'Sides, I been sick the last few days," the farmer said, adding a weak cough for emphasis. "You check with my wife if y'all don't believe me." He curled his lip and furrowed his brow, issuing a challenge to the young deputy.

Doc Steinebeck turned his head up, curious to see where this was heading. He obviously had very little liking for the deputy or his nasty chewing habit. He thought, *Wouldn't this be interesting if the old guy really got the lawman's goat? Or maybe things could get physical? That would be interesting!*

The old farmer was squinting at the deputy, his right eye nearly shut. His nostrils and long nose hairs flared out with each breath. To make matters worse, the old farmer's faded John Deere hat had fallen askew and was perched nearly sideways on his head. It gave him the appearance of a pouting five-year-old, his arms crossed over his chest and his bony elbows pointed outward.

The vet had to bite down on the inside of his cheek to keep from laughing out loud.

Deputy Dorcy simply sighed again. He wasn't going to get into it with this old timer. It just wasn't worth his time. He'd already wasted enough of the morning way out here in the sticks. If only the horse had dropped dead a mile east, it would be Grand Traverse's problem, not his.

Rather than follow up on the old man's potential alibi for a potential misdemeanor and a potential mile-long headache, Dorcy returned to scribbling in his notebook.

"What 'bout my horse?" the farmer stammered loudly. "Whatchoo gonna do 'bout it, deputy?" The old man wasn't about to leave it be.

Just like a bulldog, thought Doc Steinebeck, again biting down hard to keep from laughing. *The old guy's got a grip and won't let go. Good for him!*

Dorcy had an answer this time. With strained patience, he flipped the little notebook shut and returned it and the pen to his pocket. "Gents, let's get serious here. We ain't gonna be tying up the crime lab with some animal. The folks in Grayling, not to mention the sheriff, would have my hide if I was a-sendin' this here horse in for an autopsy."

"Then what's gone and killed my horse?" the indignant farmer hollered into the still quiet of the morning. His hands were now balled into fists, clenched at the sides of his worn-out overalls. "Somethin's done it, and somebody owes me big time."

The vet looked down at the flattened grass for a few moments, lost in thought. Then he peered up at the other two and shrugged his shoulders. "I can't saaaay what's done killed the horse, but I caaan give yous a cause of death."

When the vet wasn't immediately forthcoming, both of his companions nearly shouted at him, "What?"

Doc Steinebeck carefully removed his glasses and wiped them with his handkerchief. Then he looked up at the two men. "It's done died of fright," he said flatly.

***

A light cloud of dust particles floated up in the shaft of sunlight shining through the windows. Already it was stifling hot, even though it was barely past noon. Both teenage girls were sweating lightly even though they were more on break than actually working.

"I can't believe we have to pull kitchen duty this weekend," Julie whined. She'd been moping around the music camp's enormous kitchen for most of the morning, aimlessly tossing dish towels in between restocking the myriad of cupboards. "I just can't believe it."

Linda Hammond looked up from her inventory list and bit her lip. She wasn't going to say anything. She'd been good all morning, enduring Julie Parker's endless parading and bellyaching. She hadn't said anything yet, but her best friend here at camp was really starting to get on her nerves. She liked Julie a lot, but enough was getting to be enough. Linda didn't know how much more she could take before she'd explode.

Green Lake Music Camp wasn't really much of a camp, per se. Now, true, the campus was situated right on the north shore of Green Lake, within walking distance of both downtown Interlochen and the state park. And students stayed right at the camp for six straight weeks during the summer. Yes, every day they all wore identical green polo shirts emblazoned with Green Lake's logo. But that was where the resemblances ended.

There was no real camping that occurred, nor were there many (if any) camping activities going on, traditional or otherwise. No one ate s'mores, no one hiked the trails around the twin lakes, and no one sat around camp fires. In fact, there was almost no down time or unstructured time all week long. And campers were actually discouraged from going anywhere near the lakes for fear of catching "swimmer's itch."

Linda was pretty sure it was all a ploy by the staff to encourage the campers to spend every waking moment learning about, thinking about, talking about, or practicing music.

The campers, or music students if one were being technical, slept in nice, comfy beds in dormitories. There was no luxury of air conditioning, but each room was complete with electrical outlets into which the students plugged TVs, radios, and box fans to keep them cool. The lounge on the first floor was complete with an air hockey table, a foosball table, a pool table, and a Coke machine.

It was a far cry from real camping.

"To think, we could have been shopping up in Traverse City today. The last real weekend of camp, and we're stuck here in this sweatshop. It's not fair," Julie pouted.

The weekends were the only exception to the camp's highly structured schedule. Students were given leave to have a few hours of fun in nearby Traverse City. But one weekend during camp, each student was required to put in a few hours of what the camp declared "service time." At least the girls weren't scrubbing the dining room floor or painting the door and window frames in the dorms.

Linda only nodded, biting her lip again. She was going to have to say something really soon or Julie would go on forever. It wasn't as if Linda enjoyed the kitchen duty either. But this was what all of her weekends were like. Unlike her good friend, she spent much of her "camp leave" working anyway. And this kitchen duty was easier and far less stressful than her other job.

She didn't have many friends here at camp, at least those whom she'd like to hang out with on the weekends. She didn't particularly enjoy shopping, nor did she really have the extra money for it. Down time only allowed her thoughts to wonder back to home, and she was here at camp primarily to escape that place.

Work was better because, regardless of how mundane the job, she was distracted. She didn't have to think about her family.

Working in the camp's kitchen was better than cleaning over at the Tuscarora Club. That huge, empty lodge gave her the creeps. And despite having to listen to Julie drone on and on, at least the company here was infinitely better. The couple of old men who did hang around the lodge smoking cigars and drinking expensive golden liquor out of short glasses were always eyeing her as she cleaned and dusted. Every time she turned around, she could feel their eyes crawling around her skin. Once, she'd caught one of them staring at her unabashedly. But when she had given him an accusing glare back, she'd received a haughty, greedy, toothy leer. The worst part was that she thought he might have been drooling, too. To this day, her stomach churned when that memory returned. Nasty, dirty old men.

Julie, lost in her own world of self-pity, rattled on. "I can't believe I missed his concert in Kalamazoo in April. That was so unfair of my parents." She scrunched up her lip and nose. "It was only a few drinks. I mean, come on, it's not like they didn't drink when they were my age, too, you know."

Yeah, your life is so terrible, thought Linda. Without looking up, she said, "It was only a concert. It's not like he won't be back around again soon. He's always on tour, and you know there's a concert in Michigan or someplace nearby every year."

"But you know how much I love Elvis!" Julie said. "And 'specially since the show was right downtown. It was so close I coulda almost walked there and back." A dark cloud quickly covered Julie's otherwise beautifully round face. "It makes me so mad that *she's* going to see the King in concert back home in Syracuse the day after camp's over."

"Hasn't he cancelled all of his summer concerts so far?" Linda asked, avoiding the trap Julie had set. What Julie really wanted was to vent about Melinda Berrymore, her arch-rival at camp.

Though Linda wasn't as huge an Elvis fan as Julie, she was, after all, into music. She was walking the fine line here. If Elvis cancelled his next couple of shows, Melinda would miss out. But, of course, the King had been rather unhealthy lately, a fact that hadn't escaped Julie's enraptured attention. A sick Elvis wouldn't necessarily pull Julie out of her funk either.

Julie scowled. "No, there just weren't any shows in July. I did hear he was kinda sick, but you know he'll come out of it. He always does." She brightened up a little and dreamily said, "He is the King, you know."

"So this has nothing to do with Elvis. You're jealous that Melinda gets to see him and you don't. Face it," Linda said, unable to hold back the rising tide any longer, "You don't like Melinda 'cause she's rich."

Julie took it much better than Linda thought. "It's not so much that she has all sorts of money, or that she leads the shopping parade every weekend, or that she gets dropped off and picked up by a limousine."

Linda stared at her friend, her eyebrows up, waiting for Julie's explanation.

"It's not even that she gets everything she wants. It's just that she shoves it in my face all the time. And here we are, on a gorgeous Saturday afternoon stuck here in the kitchen. Face it, Linda," Julie said resignedly, arms crossing her chest, "We're losers."

"We are not losers. You know everybody here has to put in a few hours of service time." The dam had finally broken, and Linda nearly screamed, "Quit feeling sorry for yourself. You always get the hottest guys and you're the life of every party. You're more beautiful than anybody else here, even the rich girls. And you're better than her."

Both girls resumed putting away the myriad of tin cans and boxes of food. Both were silent for almost a minute, lost in their own thoughts.

"You really think so?" Julie asked tentatively.

Linda slammed a cupboard door a bit too hard and both girls jumped. A moment later, they were both giggling.

Getting herself under control, Linda replied, "Yes, I do. And you shouldn't need me to have to tell you that."

Again, both girls silently resumed their work.

"What're you gonna do with your night off tomorrow?" Julie asked, breaking the silence. "Just think of it, no lectures, no practices, no berating music profs. Nothing until Monday morning." She tilted her head to one shoulder and dreamily sighed.

"I don't know," Linda said a bit glumly. "Probably nothing. There's nowhere to go, nothing to do."

Julie was much more upbeat. "And this week's the last week of camp. Oh, I forgot, you're staying on for the midgets, aren't you?"

Nodding, Linda pretended to check off more items on the inventory list. The "midgets," as the regular campers so affectionately referred to them, were the little kids who came for Green Lake Music Camp's final weeks each summer. They were ages 10 to 12, and they represented the future music stars who would be gracing the camp with their presence in the coming years.

One extra week of camp was one week less she'd have to spend at home. The midget week wasn't without its pains, though. Linda would have to move all of her belongings down to one of the far more rustic bunkhouses. The new lodging was much farther from the conveniences of the camp. And all four bunkhouses had to share a central bathhouse. Typically, what lukewarm water was available ran out after just a few minutes.

It's funny, Linda thought, *The youngest kids at Green Lake got the closest experience to actual camping.* She'd be responsible for a dozen little kids in her cabin. Everywhere she went, the midgets would follow her like a trail of ducklings.

An annoyingly loud singing and humming brought her back from her reverie. Linda squeezed her eyes shut in desperation. Then she slammed down a large can of applesauce upon the counter, smiling. "And will you stop hummin' that song? It's drivin' me nuts."

Julie, however, continued to strut around the long kitchen island, arms and shoulders swinging easily to the tune that was now in her head. "What, you don't like the Commodores?"

"The Commodores are okay. I just don't see your infatuation with that song," Linda said, turning her attention back to stocking the shelves. "You're singing it all the time."

"But girl, don't you know? That's my theme song! Tell me, was there ever anyone you've ever met who was more of a *brick house* than me?"

Linda didn't have to look up to start laughing lightly. She nodded her head. Yup, Jules had the figure to go with the song, all right. She was a full-figured girl who turned boys' heads everywhere she went. It was funny that the two of them were good friends. Linda thought of herself as very plain, nothing special. She was an average girl who would never stand out in a crowd. Julie had the nice tan, the good figure, and the great smile. Linda, on the other hand, was short, skinny, and really had no figure at all. Her light brown, shoulder-length hair was a contrast to Julie's deep, shining black hair that was fluffed up, becoming such the fashion now. And based on her lackluster life back home, Linda rarely had much to smile about.

Their conversation was interrupted by the squealing whine of a truck's brakes outside the kitchen's screen door.

"Lovely," Julie sighed loudly, tossing her head side to side. "Another delivery. I can't believe how much food this place goes through in just one week. It's crazy, isn't it?"

Yeah, you sure put away your share, honey, Linda thought. Some of Julie's curves were on the verge of expansion, mostly because she loved to eat. She was always nibbling on something and her dorm room was like a snack shop. Linda thought her friend's voluptuous figure would probably disappear in just a few short years.

Adding insult to injury, the delivery truck backfired, causing both girls to jump. Then they both broke out in giggles again.

However, they were soon struck speechless when they saw the deliveryman step down from the cab. He certainly didn't meet their expectations when he strolled to the back of the truck.

The young driver seemed just about their age. He was wearing a pair of oversized bib overalls but no shirt underneath. His muscles rippled as he swung the truck's tailgate down. The faded denim straps had already given him a pair of matching tan lines over his shoulders.

The driver's dark blond hair, reaching almost to his collarbones, swayed casually in the warm, westerly breeze.

Standing in the bright afternoon sunlight, he could have been a Greek god in human form.

"Oh, my God," Julie stammered, her hand covering the wide circle her mouth had made. "Will ya look at *him*."

Both girls had paused their work and were gaping out the kitchen's back screen door. The young man dropped the tailgate of the old pickup and stacked up two wooden crates. With only a little effort, he scooped up the boxes and climbed the couple of steps to the kitchen. The girls had backed up a few steps and were pretending to be back at work, shuffling a few cans around on the counter, but from a spot where they could still easily see out the door.

"Afternoon, ladies," the deliveryman said, nodding his head to them through the screen door. A few long strands of hair fell across his forehead and danced in front of his eyes. Unable to use his hands, he blew a short puff of breath up from one side of his mouth to flick the hair back.

The young man gave Linda an interested smile, tilting his head a little at her. Linda thought she'd been struck by cupid's love arrow.

"I don't suppose either of you could give me a hand here, could ya?" he said, his eyebrows raised.

Without thinking, Julie began her flirting. She hopped over to the door and held it open for him. Her hair bounced along and she gave him a demure smile, looking out from under her long eyelashes.

He hauled in the wooden crate easily through the door and set it down on the long central island. Then he handed the folded invoice to Julie. "I'm Chris. Do you two go to camp here?"

"Hi there," Linda managed to peep out.

"Yes, we're both cadets here," Julie butted her way into the conversation, picking up where Linda was unable. She was still struck nearly speechless.

"How come you ladies are stuck in the kitchen on a gorgeous day like today?" Chris asked, tilting his head a bit to the side. "You should be down at the beach."

"Same reason as you're here," Julie said back in a sassy, flirty tone. "All cadets have to put in a weekend of 'KP' sometime during the summer." She stretched her arms out to the side, pretending to be bored. "Looks like we're all workin' today."

Having stacked the first two crates on the counter, Chris was out the door again in a flash. Both girls looked at each other and mouthed the word "hot" at the same time. Both put their hands over their mouths to keep from giggling again.

A few moments later, he was back at the door with another armload. Julie held it open and began her flirting again. But despite her best attempts, the deliveryman seemed more focused on Linda. He gave her a huge smile, his face lighting up.

Linda wasn't sure exactly what to do. This was awkward for her. No boy had ever been more interested in her than in her friend; no boy had ever resisted Julie's flirting. And this guy was something out of a dream! But despite her embarrassment, and her first inclination to look down or look away, she found it easy to stare back into his bluish-gray eyes.

Chris said, "I'm a counselor at Camp Doubennet during the week, but I work for my aunt on weekends. That's her truck. She owns Natural Harvester, the cherry company. I get the fun of delivering cherry products all over on Saturday afternoons and Sunday mornings."

"Don't you have little campers to look after?" Julie asked, the tease evident in her voice. He'd already brought in the four crates indicated on the invoice, and she wanted to keep him here talking as long as possible.

"We just finished up the last week of camp, so they all headed home this morning. We put in a few hours for some basic clean up and then we have free time until Monday morning. Next week we winterize the camp when there's no kids around."

Finally finding something to say, Linda asked, "How come you aren't on free time? Obviously you're here working when you could be down at the beach."

"I gotta save up every dime I can," Chris replied, pretty much ignoring Julie at this point. "Camp's not bad, but I gotta work every hour I can. I got a car payment and I'm saving ahead for college tuition next year. Money doesn't grow on trees, you know."

"You're still in high school?" Julie asked astonished. He looked much older.

Chris flushed momentarily. "Yup, I'll be a senior this year. I turn 18 in October. Why? How old are you two?"

"We both graduated this past spring," Julie answered. "I'm going to Western, and Linda here's going to Cornell."

Chris raised his eyebrows and nodded his head, obviously impressed. "Nice work."

Now it was Linda's turn to blush. She tried to busy herself by opening the crates Chris had just brought in. She began pulling out a number of jars and bottles while Julie checked them off the invoice.

"Here, let me help," Chris said, moving to Linda's side.

They both reached into the crate at the same time and their fingers met. Linda thought she felt a shock run right up her arm and through her body. It was like getting a chill, but it was so nice. And the best thing was that Chris didn't pull his fingers away.

They locked eyes for a long moment and Linda actually smiled.

"Well, everything's accounted for," Julie said, interrupting the moment.

Chris sighed. "Guess I'd better get going. Got a lot more deliveries to make. You guys're near the top of my list, so I've still got a full afternoon ahead of me."

He nodded to the two girls, but his attention lingered on Linda. "Nice to have met you. Maybe I'll see you around," he said with a smile.

"Yeah, maybe," Linda replied, returning her own smile. *I do hope so*, she thought.

CHAPTER 3
Distress

Father Tony stared in disbelief at the sight before him. He'd awaken early, being that it was Sunday morning. Morning prayer and daily rosary were done, as usual, in his small, cloistered room. But rather than preparing for morning mass at the Traverse City cathedral, Father Tony had packed his briefcase and climbed into the church's small sedan.

Sunday morning meant 10:30 a.m. mass in Almira at the little church in the woods. The small, country parish served around 200 year-round residents in the Lake Ann area, and in the summer, the little church would be packed for its one mass each week.

Father Tony reached the church just before nine, refreshed by the beautiful drive along North Long Lake Road. Sure, it took a bit longer than traveling directly on US-31. But the scenery was well worth it. Only a few wisps of pure white clouds dotted the beautiful blue sky. A breeze rippled through the leaves of the oaks, maples, and aspens, and as the road curved past the shore of Long Lake, similar ripples could be seen on the water's surface. The sun, already rising high, shimmered on the little waves, turning them into a sea of sparkling gold. Two swans slowly padded their way along the shallows, occasionally dipping a long neck into the water in search of breakfast.

Such inspiration always made for great homilies.

Arriving well before the parishioners, Father Tony parked in the shade of the encroaching woods on the side of the building. He grabbed his briefcase from the front seat and headed for the front entryway of the church. Still thinking of his sermon for mass, he stopped in the gravel parking lot and looked up at the familiar building.

His jaw dropped open and his eyes widened as anger was instantly replaced by a mixture of wonder and fright.

Someone's vandalized my church, he thought. *Who would do such a thing?* The flush of anger darkened his spirit. But this was only for a moment. The priest set his bag down and moved to the first of three steps leading up to the doors. As his heart began racing, Father Tony's left hand rose of its own accord and covered his mouth.

Something had created a long series of marks all along the doors, the door jambs, and the wooden siding on the front of the church.

There was a pattern to the marks; they ran in streaks of four, basically equidistant from each other. Some were straight and others curved in what would otherwise be graceful arcs.

Crossing himself, Father Tony forced himself to walk up the other two steps and reach out to the doors. The wind had died down, and there was virtually no noise to be heard except for his own harsh breathing. Despite the heat already building this early morning, the father shivered from his shoulders down to his legs.

Spreading his slightly shaking fingers, the priest traced the curving path of the scratches on one wooden entry door. Each cut was as wide as his fingernail. And these scratches weren't just superficial; they dug almost a half inch deep into the wood siding.

This wasn't an act of vandalism. These are claw marks, he thought incredulously. *Something has clawed up my church.*

This was followed closely by, *What could have created claw marks like these?*

The claw marks were all over the front of the church, scraping in crisscrossed patterns over the wooden doors. But the most disturbing aspect was how high the marks went. The Almira church was an old building, probably erected in the early 1900s. It shared the same architectural style as many churches built at that time in rural America. In particular, the tall double entry doors curved upward, meeting together at a point nearly eight feet over the stoop.

The gashes were quite visible in the siding almost a foot above the top of the door jamb.

Standing at just less than six feet tall himself, and keeping his feet flat on the concrete stoop, Father Tony could just reach the point where the doors met. He could hardly breathe.

The claw marks were still quite a bit higher.

The father forced his shaking right hand upward. It took considerable effort because his mind kept telling him, *This is wrong, terribly wrong, how could something reach this far up? It would have to be much taller than I am.*

Suddenly spooked, Father Tony swung his torso around and pressed his back against the flat doors. His eyes and head darted back and forth to the woods, visible on either side of the church. The breeze chose that moment to pick back up. Leaves and branches, as well as the tall grasses on the far side of the desolate country road, danced, their movements only further concealing what might be lurking in the shadows beyond.

He had no idea how he would explain this to the parishioners who would be arriving within the hour.

***

Unseen by the good father, a long, dark blue sedan sat parked at the road's side about 50 yards away from the church. The basic black-on-white license plates indicated it was property of the U.S. Government, though there was no agency affiliation showing on the vehicle. The driver, a plain-faced man who could have been anywhere from his mid twenties to his late forties, was the kind of person who could disappear into a crowd easily. Few noticed him and fewer still could recognize him later on. He had a knack for blending in; that was part of his job.

He carefully studied the defaced church through a pair of high-powered binoculars, then set them down and put his black, aviator-style sunglasses back over his eyes. He scribbled a series of observations on a pocket notebook, and for good measure followed this up by speaking softly into a microcassette voice recorder. Once finished speaking, he drew a circle on a county topographic map indicating the exact location of the church.

The morning was already heating up, but this government man hardly noticed it despite his white shirt and tie and black suit jacket. It was his job not to sweat.

As the first cars began arriving for early mass, the mysterious man slowly drove on by the scene, marking it well. He'd be back for a closer analysis later on that day, likely after the local police had already had their own look-about. He was sure they'd be clueless as usual.

The mystery man, however, knew exactly what had caused this damage. He knew it well. It was what brought him to northern Michigan in the first place.

***

Chris pulled the old International pickup around the back of the Boar's Head bar. He whipped it in a little fast, and a large cloud of dust rose up through the entire dirt and gravel parking lot that surrounded the rectangular building. It was still too early for customers, which was good because the dust hung in the hot morning air, refusing to settle back down. It might only be 11 a.m., but Chris was sure it was already nearly 90 degrees out.

Of course, it didn't make much sense to open the bar before noon on Sunday anyway.

Church crowd's gonna be a-sweatin' this morning, he thought.

The delivery truck nimbly backed up between a large dumpster and a pallet of beer boxes to stop a few feet from the building's rear door. Chris cut the engine, and the International backfired on cue. *Same as always*, Chris laughed to himself.

Suddenly, the back door of the bar flew open, creaking on its rusty hinges. It swung all the way until it banged off the cinderblock wall. Exiting the bar was the largest man Chris had ever met. The giant's head just barely cleared the top of the doorway, and he had to turn slightly sideways so his shoulders could make it through. The bartender resembled more of a bear than a man. His big, bushy beard covered his face and cheeks. A full head of thick, bushy hair (which added another couple of inches of height) spilled out in all directions.

"Man, can't you keep the dust down?" the gigantic man hollered, one beefy arm crossing his mouth while the other waved about in a frantic gesture, trying in vain to clear the air. "You're killin' me, bro."

The giant was dressed like a demented biker. He wore faded, black jeans and a white t-shirt with the sleeves cut off. On the top was a black leather Harley-Davidson vest which showed off his arms, each the size of a ham. Each massive, muscular arm was filled with tattoos, though Chris appreciated two the most. On the right bicep was the head of a wide sledgehammer, upon which was written OUT COLD. On the left bicep was a pickaxe with the words SUDDEN DEATH written on it. It was said around town that one punch from Tina could send a man to his grave.

Chris smiled a huge, all-American smile. "Hey, Tina, how's it hangin'?" He stuck out his right hand to the giant.

Luckily, Chris knew that Tina was really a gentle giant, and that the bartender abhorred violence unless absolutely necessary. Mostly, Tina used his intimidating size and appearance to stave off bad situations that might happen in his bar. But Chris had also heard that the gigantic man had once been a fighter in the Golden Gloves, and had never been beaten. In fact, the rumor was that he'd actually killed an opponent in the ring once, and that he'd given up fighting right then and there.

"I'm good, my man, I'm good," Tina replied, engulfing Chris' hand. Tina was almost a foot and a half taller then the young deliveryman. "But, man, you gotta keep the dust down 'round here. You know I ain't got the money to pay that little pencil-neck kid next door to come wash down the building every day. And you know how bad the dust is for my flowers, man."

The handshake slipped and moved as the two gripped fists, then bumped forearms, and then finally slapped each other five. The handshake of brotherhood, Tina always called it, though Chris's palm always stung a little from the big man's unintended grip and slap.

"I'm sorry, man," Chris replied. He knew how much Tina loved the flowers. He'd once told Chris that he wished he had been a florist. Tina had planted the colorful arrangements in the window boxes himself, and he watered them religiously each day before the lunch crowd showed up.

"Whatchoo got today, bro?" Tina asked

"Just what you ordered, big feller," Chris answered, dropping the tailgate. He reached in and pulled a wooden crate forward. It was stamped with his aunt's Natural Harvester logo.

Even though it took both hands for Chris to lift the crate, Tina snagged it with just one massive paw. "I got it, man," the bartender said. "Come on in and grab a Coke."

Unlike the other deliveries Chris had to make between Saturday night and Sunday morning, the Boar's Head was the only place that tipped. Granted, Tina only gave him a free Coke each week, but it was better than nothing. Most of Chris's stops were to ornery shopkeepers who looked down at a high school kid making deliveries. Most of them would just as soon spit on him as talk to him. But Tina was different. Tina had a heart that easily matched his great stature.

Tina gently laid the crate on the kitchen's prep counter while Chris walked over to snag two Cokes from the fridge.

"Hey, man," Chris heard Tina whine from across the kitchen. "You didn't bring any cherry vinaigrette. You know that's my favorite, man."

Chris looked back at the giant who was already putting away the various jars and cans. The young man slipped into the walk-in cooler and yelled back, "You didn't order any this week. You usually make it through two weeks, man, so I didn't think you'd need any until next Sunday."

The Cokes weren't where they were normally were, just inside the door. It took him a few moments to search the shelves until he found the cases stacked toward the back.

"I know, I know, I just been eatin' a lot of salad lately, what with all this hot weather," Tina replied, suddenly right next to him.

Chris jumped. "Man, how do you sneak around like that, being so big? You about gave me a heart attack!"

Tina just shrugged his shoulders, gave the young man a huge grin, and handed him a bottle opener. "It's too hot to sit outside. It's much better in here, man," Tina said leaning against the steel cooler shelf so his head wouldn't hit the ceiling. If the shelf wasn't up against the wall, Chris was sure that Tina would have tipped it over easily.

Chris nodded in agreement. Normally, they'd sit on the back stoop and down their sodas. This Sunday morning, however, the intense heat was best beaten right where they were. Chris's ignored his impending sense of claustrophobia, undoubtedly a result of sharing the small walk-in cooler with a man who easily took up half of the space. It might be tight quarters, but at least it was cold.

The big bartender looked down at his guest, a full two heads shorter than him. "You're a bit jumpy today. Are you spooked by that noise at night, too, man?"

"You been hearin' it, too? Way over here?" Chris asked, popping the caps from the glass bottles. He handed one to Tina who downed half of it in one swallow.

The big bartender shivered, and not from the cold. "Yea, man, everyone's talkin' 'bout it. Haven't heard much this weekend, but last week, whew! It gives me the chills, I tell you."

Both took swigs off their Cokes, savoring the sweet rush of liquid sugar.

"How's the Cherry Lady doin' with all that noise?" Tina went on, concern evident in his voice.

Chris pondered this for a few silent moments. "She hasn't mentioned it at all, come to think of it. It's funny how sometimes we don't really talk. I just come in and get to work, you know? Sometimes she just doesn't say too much."

"Except when she's tellin' stories, man," Tina said, nodding his head in recollection. "She always has the best stories."

"Yeah, I know. Sometimes I can't tell if she's makin' 'em up or not. They all sound so real when she tells 'em."

Tina clinked his bottle against Chris's. "I hear ya, bro. That lady's just got a knack for storytellin'. It's like fishin—she hooks ya and then reels ya in. I'd imagine she can spin some great campfire tales."

"That reminds me, you gonna do a bonfire tonight?" asked Chris. Tina was known for throwing bonfire parties almost every weekend out in the woods. He always seemed to have a new location, just in case things got a little wild or crazy. Not that they were big parties; generally, folks showed up by invite only. But Chris remembered one time a year ago when word got out, a couple of people invited their friends who invited their friends and so on. Before long, a couple of hundred people had invaded the campground at the nearby state forest. The DNR wasn't exactly happy.

"Naw, I'm thinkin next Sunday. I'm really bushed, man. It's been a hard week, what with all that howlin' at night. Even I'm havin' trouble dozin' off, and you know I can sleep like a rock. Bar closes at nine Sundays. Tonight I'm hopin' to be home and out by 11."

"I hear that," Chris agreed. "Old Champ thinks it's some kind of animal, maybe a bear or something, that's just lost its way." He gave Tina a wide grin. "It's on vacation maybe."

Something struck a chord with the big bartender. Tina, just finishing the last of his bottle, laughed and wheezed, spraying Coke all over the wall of the cooler.

"Well, I guess I better get goin'," Chris said glumly, "Though I'd just as soon stay here in the cooler all day. You gonna let me out?"

"Oh, yeah man, no problem. It's tough being big, you know? I forget about my size sometimes."

Chris rolled his eyes upward and gave the big man a crooked grin. "Yeah, right."

The two sauntered back into the heat of the Boar's Head's kitchen and set their empty glass bottles on the counter. Both men had to rub their eyes a bit to adjust to the bright morning sunlight. Chris and Tina slapped five as the young man headed for his truck. "Be seein' ya next week, same time, same place."

"What it is, bro, what it is," the bartender said.

***

Crickets chirped, long and lonely into the late northern Michigan night. Since the temperature hadn't really decreased as night fell, the chirping from these insects only maintained its rapid rate. Some folks could easily sleep through such a clamor piercing the otherwise calm and peaceful night.

Linda, however, lay awake on her bunk staring up at the pine boards of the ceiling. It was far too hot for covers, and she had just her bare feet tucked under the sheet.

Why would I be falling for this guy? I've only just met him yesterday, and even that was only for a few minutes, she thought. *Besides, he's only 17. He's still got a year of school left.*

You gotta stop this, Linds, she tried to tell herself. *You've got college ahead of you. An Ivy League school isn't going to give you time for boys. It'll be hard enough going through classes, let alone making the orchestra. You know how competitive it's going to be. There's no time for anything else. Besides, you don't even know if he's interested in you.*

He seemed interested, she argued back at her thoughts.

If something happens, it happens.

And if something were to happen? There's not much left of summer up here, but who really knows?

A little shaft of moonlight crept into the little cabin's window, illuminating the bare wooden floors. Looking that direction, she could see a few bugs buzzing their merry way along the window screen. And still those crickets kept on chirping. It didn't matter; she had too much on her mind to sleep anyway.

She wondered again if the pressure was getting to her. She thought back, years back, to her mother pushing her to earn all A's. She could still recall that day

"You don't have time for TV," her mother chastised her. "You need to practice if you're going to be the best. You need to study if you're going to get the best grades."

Her one rebellion, her only rebellion, had occurred when she was a freshman. She abandoned the flute for drums. It was a crushing blow to her mom. Playing flute was her mother's fascination. And Linda was good at it. But there was a calling from the percussion, a deep almost primeval summoning. It had always called to her from the first time she'd listened to music. But her mother forced her to the flute.

With her skill in music (*A dozen years, honey,* she reminded herself), she'd picked up the drums immediately. She was an expert in a month's time.

Her mother hated it. She of course blamed everybody and everything. It was her friends (Linda wasn't allowed to have them over anymore). It was the things she did (Linda was all but grounded at home permanently). It was her classes (Mom pestered the school administration until they reluctantly promoted her to the highly selective honors classes, which of course meant more work and more pressure).

Perhaps it was coming out of that middle school "who cares" attitude that brought it on. Maybe it really was the inspiration of all of the rebellions her friends created with their families.

But she thought maybe she'd just had enough.

The one thing her mother hadn't taken away was camp. Camp was still sacred. But camp was also safe—all music, all the time, and no other distractions.

And yet, she loved music. It was her life. It was all she dreamed about.

Except now, you're also dreaming of that boy, she thought.

His face flashed across her mind from their last meeting. His dark blond hair was a little too long and a little unkempt—you could tell it hadn't been cut all summer. He was athletic—it was in the way he moved, the way he walked.

He had touched her shoulder, just in passing, and she nearly jumped out of her skin.

Gritting her teeth, she stifled a cry. *Why is life so unfair?* she nearly screamed inside her head. Her hands were in fists pushing down into the uncomfortable mattress. *I finally get things all set and now this.* She reached behind her, grabbed her thin pillow, and pressed it against her face. Her muffled scream was almost totally lost in the fabric. Almost lost, anyway.

A voice in the dark made her jump. She nearly screamed again, but this time it was from being scared.

"Wha's goin' on?" a sleepy voice posed in the darkness. It wasn't really that loud, but it was totally unexpected.

Now real anger flashed through her. She hated being spooked.

"Amy, go back to sleep," she all but barked across the bunk room. *Midgets*, she cursed in her head. *First day and they're already on my nerves.*

A set of bed springs creaked and there was a rustle of sheets, but no more voices.

Linda patiently waited for her heart to stop pounding. When she was finally calmed down, she returned to her previous thoughts, after being so rudely interrupted. *No, Linds, you just gotta let it go. You don't have time for this. Just let him go.*

And yet, when she did finally fall asleep, that young delivery guy was in her dreams again.

CHAPTER 4
Ogopogo

The canoe slipped uneasily through the tall grass growing out of the nearly still water. The aluminum watercraft's pointed bow pushed aside the great green blades only temporarily; they sprang back tall and upright after the canoe passed, hiding its course completely. No one could have guessed that anyone had come that way at all.

Though the Betsie River's current was still strong someplace in the depths of the mire, it wasn't apparent to the paddlers.

"Man, my arms are killing me from all this paddling," Fred O'Bryant whined from the canoe's front seat. He laid his paddle across his lap. Water droplets fell from the paddle's blade back into the green hue of the river. "What's it been now, an hour? We shouldn't be havin' to work this hard to head downstream, you know."

"The current's here," Ed O'Bryant replied from the rear of the canoe. His paddle nonchalantly switched from one side to the other, steering them clear of the largest of the grassy outcrops. "It's just a ways beneath the surface. All this tall grass diffuses the energy here at the surface. You just can't see the current. But trust me, it's down there."

The two brothers had been in the marshy area of the Betsie River for some time now. At this point, a few miles from Green Lake, the river widened out, spreading out over several hundred acres. Even the tree line, previously tight up to the river banks, had backed away. The two men had enjoyed the first hour's travel beneath the cool shade of the many overhanging branches.

However, since arriving in the marsh, the sun had beaten down upon them relentlessly. Both men's faces and necks were brightening into a rosy red. Beneath the short sleeves of their loose fitting, button-up shirts, their hairy arms were catching up quickly.

Ed's wispy hair, thinning since he graduated from high school, was luckily covered with a navy blue bandana he'd tied up in the back. Fred wasn't as lucky; his receding hairline exposed far too much forehead, which would now be peeling in less than a day.

"I wonder how deep it gets around here?" pondered Fred, wiping sweat from his brow. "I can't see more than a few inches from all the muck."

Ed thought deeply for a few seconds, peering at the marsh. A few feet away, a small, green frog leaped into the water, sending concentric circles up against the thick stalks of the grass. Then he looked up at his brother and grinned. "Don't know. Why don't you slip over the edge and check it out? I'd be willin' to bet you'd be up to your eyeballs in mud."

Fred wrinkled his nose and lip. "You couldn't pay me enough to swim here. Just think of the leeches that'd be all over you when you came up."

"If you came up," Ed said slowly. After a few moments of deep thought, he added, philosophically, "A man gets his boots stuck in that crap, he just might not make it back up. That muck just might not want to let him go."

Fred nodded silently and then shivered, despite the late afternoon's heat. There probably wasn't a worse death than to be drowned. His mind produced horrible images of being trapped below the surface—legs encased in the grip of the mud's suction, struggling for freedom; arms and fingers outstretched, reaching for the dim light above; lungs burning for air until the inevitable happened and an involuntary gulp filled them with warm mud.

"Can't see much more above than below," Ed said flatly, turning his head again from one side of the marsh to the other. "Grass has to be, what do you think, three or four feet high? I can't even tell where the river banks are."

"You think we're still on the river?" Fred asked warily. "You know, there's lots of tributaries in and out of this stretch of the Betsie. With no current to really speak of, we could be anywhere in this marsh."

"Man, just relax," Ed replied, a little annoyed at his brother. "I'm sure we're just fine."

They'd started their voyage, just a day trip really, from Alberta's Canoe Livery outside Green Lake. Alberta, the ancient lady who ran the place, had warned them about this part of the river, the part the locals called the "Spreads." "But strong lads like y'all selves should be able to pull through, he he he," she had cackled at them, staring at them out of one squinted eye. Witch-like, she pointed one crooked and wrinkled finger at the two men. If ever there was a lady who looked the part (and sounded like a witch, too), it was old Alberta.

Ed and Fred paid their money for a six-hour adventure, and as they padded their way down the riverbank to claim their canoe, they were amazed that the old lady was waiting for them there. She hardly seemed able to scoot herself around the little office. And yet, she had already wrangled the 16-foot aluminum canoe into position, loaded it with paddles and life jackets, and had not even broken a sweat in the 90-degree afternoon temperatures.

As they slid the canoe into the brown, muddy water, old Alberta cackled again. "Keepa lookout fer wildlife out yonder," she said to the two brothers again with one eye tightly squinted. "We've been a-hearin' some un-yoooosual noises of late 'round these parts."

The two brothers who dwarfed the tiny, ancient woman first looked at each other and then back down to Alberta. She stared at them in a serious repose for a few more seconds and then broke out in her evil-sounding cackle again. Ed and Fred joined her, laughing uneasily a few moments later.

"Some funny feller left just 'fore you guys done came in. Musta been a tourist, I reckon. Sure didn't fit in round these parts, wearin' his dark sunglasses indoors and all. He was a-askin' lotsa questions 'bout that howlin' at night. Not that I had any answers for him, mind ya."

"Can't imagin' you two big, strappin' boys being 'fraid of much, though, nope I can't," she said thoughtfully. "But yer muscles'll be sore an' tired tonight, I guarantee-ya, after diggin' through the 'Spreads,' that's fer sure."

Starting their way into the strong pull of the river current, the two heard the old woman cackling again, her loud shrill voice echoing through the forest behind them.

Out here in the "Spreads," the Betsie River dam was wholly responsible for their slow going, of course, and it hadn't taken long for the river to overspill its banks and spread its way all over the lowlands in this part of Grand Traverse County. The result was the wide marsh in which the two brothers now found themselves entangled.

However, they were both startled a moment later when a long, low cry echoed across the waterway.

"What the blazes was that?" Fred squeaked. His eyes were darting from one side to the other.

The shrill cry came again, long and slow, though neither brother could tell from which direction it originated. Fred's weight was dangerously forward in the canoe as he peered into the jungle of weeds.

Suddenly, water splashed up at the right side of the canoe, soaking Fred's sleeve. He cried out in surprise.

Ed chuckled loudly, then hit the water's surface a second time with the broadside of his paddle, splashing his brother and soaking most of his shirt and shorts.

Fred jerked around in the seat, rocking the canoe. "What was that for?" he shot back at his brother angrily, even though the cold water felt great on his hot skin.

"It's just a loon, you moron," Ed said, hiding his own momentary brush of fear. "Haven't you ever heard one before?"

Fred was amused neither at his brother's antics nor at his apparent depth of knowledge. "As a matter of fact, no, I haven't. And how, may I ask, would you know what a loon sounds like?"

Ed tried to impress his younger brother with his obvious years of experience. He rolled his eyes in resignation. "Man, you gotta get out more. Now I've heard loons..."

But he was cut off by another splash, this time from his brother's paddle. Fred had slapped the river's surface with great enthusiasm, sending a blast of water to the rear of the canoe. Ed's shirt and shorts were instantly soaked and rivulets of water streamed down his face and over his handlebar mustache, which now stuck to his cheeks and lips. The older brother sputtered a few times, blinking his eyes in surprise while spraying river water from his lips. He looked like a drowned rat.

Fred couldn't help laughing out loud, a great belly laugh that nearly upset the canoe a second time. He almost lost his paddle as his arms crossed his paunchy stomach.

Like his brother a few seconds earlier, Ed actually felt better from the cool splash. If they'd been out in the river proper, he'd have slipped overboard and had a refreshing swim. However, here in the murky swamp, it wasn't just impractical, but it was potentially dangerous. In the meantime, he'd just have to enjoy the momentary relief from the heat with a little play.

Over the next two minutes, a battle ensued between the front and back seats of the watercraft. Ed and Fred slapped the water's surface with their paddles, spraying water in all directions as if they were teenagers again. They howled with laughter and a few well-aimed curses at each other, breaking up the quietude of the wilderness around them.

They were utterly alone on the river. The only folks who canoed on Tuesday afternoons were the Boy Scouts from the nearby summer camp, and they'd all gone home two weeks ago.

There was no one anywhere nearby to hear the clamor they made, no people for miles around.

But there was something else in the vicinity that did hear them. From its resting place in the forest beyond the river's edge, it heard them very well.

By the time the melee was over, the brothers were both soaked and fully refreshed. Ed's bandana dripped water down his cheeks as little droplets began evaporating. They rested in their seats, both almost out of breath.

However, their moment of merriment was lost as another loud cry echoed through the swampy wilderness. But unlike the loon's call, this new sound was deep and sinister, an awful shriek that seemed to carry on for an eternity. In reality, it only lasted about 10 seconds but neither brother noticed.

It was as if time had stopped along with all other noises around them. There was no chirping or squawking from the birds, no peeping or croaking from the frogs. Even the very light breeze stopped. Not a leaf or branch moved. The few wispy clouds made a painting high above, like stretched cotton candy on a baby-blue tablecloth. The sun continued to beat down, oppressing the land with its heat. Everything in nature had paused, waiting in anticipation, hiding itself from this new and awful menace that had invaded it. Seemingly, the world had inhaled deeply and was holding its breath, waiting for what was coming next.

Both men stopped their motion and absolutely froze in their canoe. Neither spoke, neither could breathe. A few drops of water fell, plopping their way slowly into the dead still marsh below. The canoe stopped its forward motion and came to a rest amid another clumping of swamp grass.

The only sound to invade the silence was the light buzzing of a few deer flies and a small cloud of mosquitoes that made its way to the canoe in search of lunch. Ed slowly waved his hand past his right ear and long sideburns, absently brushing aside one of the bloodsuckers.

The words that escaped Fred's throat were raspy and barely audible. "Heh, heh, loon...right?" he sputtered, half hopeful yet wholly uneasy.

The noise came again, this time a deeper, darker, far more awful growl. Both men turned their heads simultaneously to the left, peering at the copse of trees and thickly overgrown underbrush barely visible over the tops of the tall swamp grass. The forest and the swampy river appeared to meet at what seemed to be about 50 yards away. The menacing, guttural growl was definitely coming from that direction. A half-dozen black birds, crows probably, burst out of the tree tops and flew off in all directions.

Fred's knuckles were white, his fingers holding a death grip on the paddle's shaft. "Man, whatever that was, it wasn't no loon," he whispered, just barely heard by his brother.

Both brothers sat silently, not moving, not making a sound.

Ed only nodded his head. "I think maybe we ought to start paddlin' again. Slowly, quietly."

At the front of the canoe, Fred silently dipped his paddle in the river first on one side and then the other. The canoe slipped forward without a sound. But their progress seemed to be slower and slower as the tall grasses and reeds thickened around them. They tried changing directions several times, turning one way and then the next. Fred's paddle spent more time pushing away the vegetation than propelling them through the water.

"Hey, steer left," Fred shot over his shoulder. "We're going to get hung up."

"I can't tell which way to go," Ed hissed back at his brother. "It all looks the same."

The two had moved perhaps 20 or 30 yards into the ever-increasing mire when the awful growl echoed across the land again. Both of their heads spun to the right. This time the noise was much closer. As they stared into the distance, both were startled by a large splash. The splash reminded Ed of doing a belly-smacker in the YMCA pool where they'd grown up. Cannonballs and watermelons were two of his favorite dives, always shooting up a tremendous spray of water. Less than a second later, the expelled water showered back into the river. Something large had obviously just entered the river.

Both brothers kept staring through the tall weeds. But the river was no longer silent. The splashing continued, and it was becoming louder and more violent as it got closer. It sounded as if something was swimming their way, struggling through the tall weeds.

"I think we should keep paddling," Fred suggested softly. His hands were already working, increasing their pace.

From the back of the canoe, Ed didn't even have to nod. He'd already matched Fred, stroke for stroke.

In the distance, the splashing grew closer and closer despite the brother's efforts to escape. Another menacing growl caused them to turn their heads backward though their arms never lost their momentum. Both were amazed to see the tall weeds moving, parting as something began to push its way through. It wasn't clearly identifiable, but its dark form seemed to belong to some kind of huge animal. From the growling, they knew it wasn't friendly. The two men begin paddling frantically trying to escape the mire and whatever was closing in on them.

"What is that?" Fred asked incredulously. "Is it a bear or something?"

"I don't care what it is," Ed responded, swinging his head forward again. "Let's get outta here! Go! Go!"

Fred's frantic paddling was nearly matched by his brother, who had the added chore of steering the watercraft. Ed used every power stroke he could muster to gently maneuver the canoe around the thickest clumps of grass. But it was their arm, chest, and back muscles that took over, forcing the canoe forward.

It was beyond time to stay silent. Their paddles splashed water in all directions as the men huffed, soon getting the workout of their lives. The splashing of the creature behind them continued to increase in volume.

"Keep paddling!" Ed yelled from the rear of the canoe. Obviously, if their pursuer caught up to them, it would reach him first. With that in mind, he pushed himself even harder.

The canoe couldn't go fast enough. It was like some horrible movie where escape seemed to be just out of reach, the distance to safety just a bit too far away. Time had slowed down, and the creature behind them closed the gap.

Despite Fred's manic paddle strokes, the canoe still had to plow its way through the thick entanglements. Even from the front seat, he could see no end to the weeds. They'd been in this mire for an hour now and who knew in which direction they were heading.

The growl erupted from behind them again, and this time they could hear the intensity of the creature's rush through the swampy, brackish water.

Fred took one more look over his shoulder and saw glimpses of their pursuer. A dark, hairy muzzle appeared first. A bit above the jaws he could see black, pointed ears up at attention. Powerful, hairy arms pushed through the water and the grasses. But what truly caught his gaze were the glowing yellow eyes, staring out, unblinking, between the blades of grass. It was these eyes, and their contrast to the dark form of the creature, that really spooked him.

The weeds were really thick, a virtual African grassland right here on the river's surface. Both brothers had to struggle to keep their paddles from becoming entangled and yet continue to propel them forward.

The growl came again, only feet behind them. Ed was sure he could feel the creature's breath on his sunburned neck and shoulders. He imagined it was a howl of triumph, and that the beast would reach out and clutch him any second now.

And then, they were free! The canoe zipped through the last cropping of river grass and slid its way easily into the fast moving flow of the Betsie River. With both brothers paddling like mad, the canoe certainly lived up to its aerodynamic design. Aided by the current and not impeded by the tall reeds, the canoe shot downstream. Despite aching muscles, both men kept paddling like there was no tomorrow.

There was no looking back for Fred. His muscles strained as he plunged the paddle deeply into the river, moving it quickly from one side of the canoe to the other. His mind was totally blank, and the flight instinct had completely taken over.

Ed, on the other hand, took one last glance over his shoulder, his arms continuing their maddening strokes. A few feet behind the edge of the tall grass he could see the creature staring at them. It was submerged up to its wide, hairy shoulders. Its eyes glowed despite the late afternoon sun. The thick tangle of river weed couldn't totally hide the beast's form—its pointed ears; its long, doglike muzzle; its lips that seemed to be curled up in an almost human grin.

My God, what is that thing? he thought. *And how could it be grinnin' at me?*

Somehow it looked too much like old Alberta's parting grin as they left the livery. It was far too human of a face for a wild animal to make.

That last bit was too much for the older brother. Ed swung his head back to the front and paddled like his life depended on it.

His life, in fact, did.

***

Now that the campers were gone, there really wasn't much to do out at Camp Doubennet in the evenings. Champ had no problem lending his car to Chris so the young man could put in a few hours each night over at Natural Harvester. Chris was friends with the other counselors who stayed during the extra cleanup week and he'd love to hang out with them, but he knew his aunt could also use all the help she could get, especially this time of year. And there was always a great dinner to look forward to. Not that camp food was all that terrible, but a hearty, home-cooked meal was a nice treat.

At the moment, he was sticking labels on glass jars at Natural Harvester. The current batch was sour cherry preserves. It was boring work, but work that needed to be done.

Reading through the latest purchase order, Brett Parsons turned to Chris and said, "Your turn to get supplies. We'll need a full lug of black cherries."

"Make it two," Natalie Robbins, Chris's aunt, said loudly over her shoulder. "You'll need it for your next order."

Chris nodded, silently. He didn't mind. Working for his aunt's cherry factory sure beat any other job he could be doing when he wasn't at camp. Besides, nobody else would hire him for half a day on Saturday and half a day on Sunday and for a few hours nightly during the week. And that was the only time he had off from Camp Doubonnet.

Brett lived at the end of the road. He'd been working for Natalie for four years, the same as Chris. The two were the same age, and as children, they spent every waking moment together when Chris came up north to visit. Once Chris became a camper and then later a camp counselor, the two had a little less time together, at least in long stretches. But they got to see each other more, now spaced out over the entire summer instead of the long days where they could get into all sorts of mischief.

And Aunt Natalie had hired him on mostly for the busy summer months. But she did find a number of jobs at the cherry factory that Brett could do to provide him some spending cash year round. He was also saving up for his own wheels. Until then, he had to borrow his dad's green Plymouth Volare sedan still. It was fairly new, but it was awful to be seen riding around in.

The boys weren't allowed in the kitchen areas where the various batches of jams, jellies, preserves, vinaigrettes, and other tasty treats were concocted. Aunt Natalie's regular staff did those jobs during the day. Brett and Chris really didn't want to be in that sweatshop anyway. The heat from the burners and the steam from the huge boiling pots and canning made that room absolutely stifling. They preferred to flex their muscles out here in the loading dock. Over the years, they'd had plenty of chances to compare their biceps.

Natural Harvester really wasn't a factory, even though that was what they called the series of buildings on Aunt Natalie's property. It would be more properly described as a warehouse. Natalie's business wasn't huge compared to many of the really big fruit companies in the four-county area surrounding Traverse City. But hers was one of the few that distributed and hand-delivered to local stores and restaurants.

"We're almost out of jam, too," Brett added, stooping to look into the lower storage cupboard. Will you bring a few cases in with you, too?"

Chris snagged the dolly and pushed it to the storehouse, wheeling around Winnie, Aunt Natalie's Yellow Lab, who was sacked out on the floor. Once in the other room, Chris stacked four cases of jam carefully on the dolly. Then he grabbed two lugs of whole cherries from the cold storage room, set them on top of the boxes of jam, and then wheeled everything back to his aunt's combination loading dock and office.

Aunt Natalie sat at her desk on the far side of the room, plodding her way through paperwork. She was surrounded by dozens of three-ring binders and wire baskets full of papers. The fingers of her left hand flew across the papers, scribbling notes, while the fingers of her right hand deftly maneuvered over the keys of a large adding machine. Several clicks were followed by a whirr as the little strip of paper exited the adding machine and wound around itself.

Every few minutes, Natalie would slip a customer order up on the clipboard that hung on the wall next to her desk. Brett would then saunter over, grab it, and take it to the stainless steel countertop where the two boys were filling orders, stacking the many bottles and cans into various-sized wooden crates. Once each crate was filled, it was stacked near the double back doors to await delivery. The boys knew not to load up the truck's bed until they had a full shipment ready to go. The cherry products, especially the fresh, whole cherries, needed to be kept out of the heat as much as possible.

"I'm telling you its *Ogopogo*," Brett said casually to Chris as he packed up another crate. "Just like those stories your aunt used to tell us when we were kids."

Chris scrunched his face a bit and tilted his head. "I don't remember her ever telling that story, and I've been coming up north all my life. What's *Ogopogo?*" he asked looking from Brett to his Aunt Natalie.

"Maybe she didn't tell you. I thought she had. Probably 'cause you're from downstate. You know, we pretty much keep our legends to ourselves up here," Brett said, giving Chris a sly smile. "But I suppose since you do come up north every summer, we can share it with you. Natalie, do you want the honor of telling him?" Brett asked.

The older woman continued scratching her pen across her papers for a few more seconds and then paused, taking a deep breath. Chris waited anxiously, hoping his aunt would tell the story. Some of Chris's best memories were of Aunt Natalie telling stories around the campfire. Everyone would be bundled up in heavy, woolen blankets, drinking hot cocoa and eating s'mores.

"The legends of *Ogopogo* go back hundreds, if not thousands, of years," she began slowly, carefully choosing her words. "I was first told about these legends from my grandmother when I was a little girl. Of course, she'd heard the stories from her own grandmother, and on and on back through history. I don't know how far back these really go, but Nana was pretty sure they were really old stories. I mean *really* old stories, like from the times of the cavemen, you know?

"Nana never could tell me exactly what *Ogopogo* meant in the Omeena tongue. I'm not sure she actually knew. But she did think that it was a very old word, and that its current pronunciation isn't exactly accurate. She's pretty sure it's close but that it has changed over time.

"Now, realize that what I'm going to tell you is only folklore, but to the people of our Omeena band, these are the closest things we have to history. And no matter how far-fetched the legends sound, there's always a grain of truth in the Omeena stories. They were not a people to create fictional stories like other tribes and cultures around the world did."

Puzzled, Chris tilted his head. "I've never heard of the Omeena band," he said. "And we studied the Michigan tribes in pretty good detail this past spring in school. I know I would have remembered that name."

"That's 'cause they don't exist any more," Natalie explained. "The Omeena were a small band of Indians not really affiliated with any major tribe in Michigan or anywhere else for that matter. They spoke a language that was a mix of both Ottawa and Ojibwa with a bit of French, English, and a few of their own words thrown in for good measure. In terms of culture, they probably resembled the many other woodland Indians of the Midwest. But there were other elements in the designs and colors of their clothing and jewelry that reminded me of tribes in the southwest or even in Mexico.

"Anyway, they lived right here in the Interlochen area. As a matter of fact, the name Interlochen comes from the Omeena word for 'between the lakes.' Of course, the French fur-traders liked to claim the town's name as their own, saying it's French, but the truth is they adapted the name from the Omeena."

Chris listened, fascinated. He'd always loved history, especially Michigan history.

"So, anyway, back to *Ogopogo*. The stories describe this legendary creature as very elusive. In fact, it is said that no one had really seen the monster and lived to tell of it."

Chris frowned. "So if no one lived, how'd the stories spread?"

"I was getting to that," Natalie said, giving him the cold, hard stare. She continued a few moments later. "There were, of course, a large number of encounters in which the Omeena people heard awful howls and screeches in the night, just like those we've been hearing lately. And there were a few stories, just a few mind you, of actual sightings. These were all from a distance away, and they were all very similar. The creature didn't notice those who'd seen it because they were hunkered down behind rocks or logs or behind large trees or something.

Those who claimed to have seen *Ogopogo* were so scared they couldn't move."

Both boys were excited now. "Tell him what it looks like, Natalie," Brett said anxiously.

Natalie smiled, knowing her tale was completely drawing them in. "Those who saw *Ogopogo*, and as I mentioned earlier, they only saw a little bit, they always describe it as walking upright like a man. But that was where the similarities ended.

"*Ogopogo* was difficult to see clearly, probably because its skin was furry or hairy, and it almost completely blended in with its surroundings. It generally was seen hunched over, many times drinking from a stream or pond. But even standing, its long arms could almost touch the ground. The face and head seemed like some sort of familiar animal, like a wolf or a bear, you know, something the native people would have seen in our area.

"But probably the creepiest thing that all of the stories have in common is about its eyes. Its eyes glowed a demonic gold, each a burning sun in the depths of its black face, even in the daylight hours."

Chris was enraptured. Even Brett, who'd heard this tale several times, couldn't help but be drawn in by it again.

"Interestingly, most stories actually describe *Ogopogo* swimming in a lake or pond," Natalie went on. "Many who've seen *Ogopogo* mistakenly think it is some sort of a sea creature, something like the Loch Ness Monster, because only its head pokes out of the water's surface. But there are a few stories from those people who were brave enough to stick around and watch the creature emerge from the water.

"One story tells of a fair maiden who was gathering berries at the edge of the forest in the early morning. She looked up over the thick bushes and saw something swimming in a nearby lake. Curious, but apprehensive, she kept down and only peered through the tangle of thorny stems and leaves. Only its head was visible. The animal swam to the far edge of the lake, and once it reached the shallows, it emerged walking out onto the shoreline. It walked upright like a human, but even from that distance she could tell it was neither man nor animal. It could only be *Ogopogo*.

"The monster turned around and looked right at the bushes where the maiden was hiding. She froze, holding her breath, not making a sound, knowing that if she did, she'd never make it back to her village. The creature took several steps in her direction, peering at her with its glowing golden eyes. But then, its ears twitched, and its head snapped around to face the opposite direction. It crouched for a moment, listening intently, before springing away into the thick forest.

"The maiden's heart beat furiously for a full minute as she forced herself to remain completely still, making sure the creature was well on its way. Then she sprinted all the way back to her village, not even stopping when her face and arms were stung by sharp branches."

Chris and Brett slowly turned their heads to look at each other. Both raised their eyebrows at the same time. *Just like little boys*, Natalie thought before going on.

"Another story tells of a young man, an Omeena hunter, who had been stalking a black bear. Now, you know that a black bear can be the most fearsome animal in the wilderness, even more so than a cougar. This hunter had been trailing the black bear for days, since a big bear in the vicinity of the village is not a good thing.

"As he followed the bear tracks, he came across a large, flattened area of ferns and shrubs. All of the ground and vegetation were stained a deep red, and there were claw marks and scrapings on the forest floor. Even a few smaller saplings had been broken or crushed. When the hunter touched it, he realized it was blood.

"His spear at the ready, the hunter noiselessly followed the trail of bloody paw prints up a rise. And there, below, he saw the huge black bear lying dead on its side, its hide torn with claw marks. The hunter swiveled his head, looking about the wilderness for what might have killed such a mighty beast. And that was when he heard the tearing, gurgling sounds coming from the underside of the bear.

"A beastly, dog-like head and clawed hands raised up over the carcass of the dead animal. The creature's teeth and muzzle were stained a bright red. It gulped down a chunk of meat and snarled at the hunter.

"The hunter knew it had to be *Ogopogo*, so, mindful of his life, he slowly backed down the rise and once he passed the clearing where the battle had taken place, he turned and ran back to his village without stopping. He traversed the four days of walking in just one afternoon. But he made it safely.

"That's the only story my Nana knew of where someone actually survived an encounter. So I guess someone *did* live to tell the tale. That is, of course, if you believe the tales."

"Wow," Chris whispered. "And do you think that it's *Ogopogo* that's been howling around here lately, Aunt Natalie?"

"It's just a myth, though," Brett said quietly. "Isn't it? I mean, that's just the kind of tale we'd tell the flatlanders."

Shrugging her shoulders, she gave him a look that wasn't exactly a smile. "I have no idea what might be making that howling. I'm not so sure I believe in *Ogopogo* now, though I did as a little girl. But these last couple of weeks haven't seemed quite normal, at least to me. It feels like an emptiness in the world around us. I'm sure you boys have noticed it, too. I don't hear as many birds or frogs or any other sorts of animals any more."

Winnie lay her head down and pushed her muzzle beneath her paws. She wined, as if she fully understood the conversation around her.

The boys both nodded. There was a noticeable lack of animal life. Chris hadn't seen any deer tracks or scat around camp. And the raccoons and opossums that always marauded the trash dumpster were nowhere to be seen.

Aunt Natalie continued. "I don't know what's going on, but something's keeping the wildlife away. I'd be willing to bet it's connected to whatever is making that god-awful noise. Whether its *Ogopogo* or not, that I don't know."

CHAPTER 5
Recognition

Old Charlie Cooper pulled his aging pickup perfectly between the freshly painted lines of the parking space. Much like the International pickup Chris drove on the weekends, Charlie's Willys Jeep Pickup sputtered and bucked a few times before its engine finally quit. The old man just chuckled, giving Chris a goofy grin that was accentuated by a number of missing teeth. "Don't make 'em like they used ta, huh?" he laughed. Chris could only smile and nod.

The two truck doors creaked open, the hinges protesting and squealing in the otherwise quiet afternoon, and Chris noticed a number of flakes of rust, some small and a few large ones, fall to the cement. Grimacing, he slammed the passenger door twice before it finally latched.

"Watch yer step, now," the old timer whispered, leaning in toward his companion. "Yer on club property. Someone's always watchin' you." With that, he pointed up at a surveillance camera mounted on a tree above them.

It was the first time Chris had been up close to the great Tuscarora Club lodge. Of course, he'd seen it from the water when he'd taken the little campers out to canoe on Lake Doubennet, and it was certainly impressive from that angle. Now, up on land, Chris was completely amazed. And it wasn't just that they had surveillance cameras all over the property.

There was a lot of money sunk into this place. A ton of money more likely. It was very obvious in every detail that Chris could see.

Rather than just the dirt or gravel road and parking area, like those found at most other homes, cottages, and resorts around Interlochen and Lake Ann, everything here was cement or pavement. Angled brick pavers formed a wide walkway up to the front of the edifice. The grounds were an artful collection of flowerbeds and well-manicured shrubs and grass, all bordered by stone ledges.

The entire building was built using huge logs, probably cedars, that were two feet or more in diameter. It was the biggest log cabin Chris had ever seen. Of course, it wasn't a simple cabin, it was a resort—basically a hotel in its own right. Dozens of windows looked down over the woods, the grounds, and as Chris knew, over the lake shore on the far side of the building.

The Tuscarora Club property butted right up to the wooded acres owned by Camp Doubennet. But down the property line between them, the club had erected a 10-foot tall steel wire fence. Each year when he returned to camp, Chris noticed the fence had been moved further and further into the camp's property. When Champ was asked about this, he only responded that he'd had to sell a "few acres" to the club. In four years, Chris guessed 50 acres or more had transferred ownership.

Facing them on the ground floor was the grand entryway. A huge wrap-around log porch, deep enough to hold full-sized picnic tables, welcomed visitors. Two wide stairs carved from half logs led up to a pair of ornately carved doors.

"Nice, huh?" Charlie said, elbowing Chris in the ribs. "Wait 'till you see the inside."

"How old is this place?" Chris asked, utterly amazed. He'd only really noticed it since he began working as a counselor four years ago. "Everything seems so new."

"Well, partly it's so nice because that old tycoon spends a pretty penny keepin' it that way. Course, the other part is that much of this whole place *is* very new. This place keeps on a-growin' every year. I swear, he'll own the entire lake in short order."

Chris looked the old timer square in the face. "Don't you think it's unusual that the people around here keep selling out to him?"

"Now I can't say for sure," the old guy croaked, "but I have my inklin's. There's been a mighty lota strange things a-goin' on over the years. Shady deals, maybe. But, Harris Wellington does have a ton of money. Part of me thinks maybe he just made 'em some very good offers. Course, there's a part of me that wonders if he was offerin' cash, you know what I mean?"

Nodding slowly, Chris understood completely. There were many ways to entice someone to sell and not all of them involved money. There was a fine line between persuasion and coercion.

"I've lived 'round these parts all my life, yessir," he went on. "Most everyone I knowed is gone now."

Charlie gave him the quick history. "There was the Woods homestead, yup, they was the first to sell out. That was, let's see, 40 acres, I think. And of course the Adams place. Their house was a-right over there." Charlie pointed at the tennis courts. "Flattened their house so they can play tennis. Can't say I ever seen anybody playing, though. Waste of money, I always thought.

"Anyhoo, fire done gutted two cabins that was owned by downstate folks. They was right down there by the lake.

Funny how those folks sold out to him rather than take their insurance and rebuild, huh?"

"Isn't it a bit suspicious how many fires there's been around here?" Chris asked.

"Naw," Charlie said rather quickly. "Most places around here are old, I mean really old. Old wiring, old plumbing, the kinda places that was a-put up 'fore building codes. Really old and dried-up places." He whistled softly between the couple of gaps in his teeth. "They's firetraps, mosta 'em, just a-waitin' for a spark. Downstate folks had bought 'em up but didn't really wanna spend much on improvements. They gotta lota respect for keepin' things the same, I guess.

"Mayhap there was some cash exchangin' hands. But I'm willin' to bet some raw deals have gone down. Too many folks have up and left. Too many folks who were permanent residents 'round here. I mean, they been here all their lives and suddenly they're up and gone, no lookin' back, no word from 'em ever. I gotta believe there's somethin' that's been a-drivin' 'em away."

The two stared off at the great lodge, taking in its grandeur.

"What do you think about that howling we've been hearing at night?" Chris asked a few moments later.

The old man slowly looked to his right and left. His eyes were a bit comical as they darted back and forth, almost expecting some monster to spring out of the woods.

Charlie lowered his voice, leaning in toward the young man and whispered, "I don't know what that thing is. I ain't heard nothin' like it in my life."

"Isn't it a coyote or a wolf or bobcat or something?" Chris asked. Of course, he kept his aunt's folklore explanations to himself.

Charlie shook his head slowly. "Nope. I've been a-hunting' for most my life round these here parts. There's no wolfs down this way anyway—theys only in the UP. Bobcats, coyotes, they don't sound nothin' like that howlin' we been a-hearin."

Chris found himself looking off into the deep forest, wondering what had been making that awful noise. Was it just some critter in the wrong place at the wrong time? Or was there perhaps some grain of truth to Aunt Natalie's stories?

"Nope, I don't know what it is. But I can tell you this," Charlie said in confidence. "It don't belong 'round here. The way it sounds, I'm not sure it belongs anywhere."

***

They were ushered into the lodge by Braydon, Mr. Wellington's personal assistant, who had looked down on the visitors with a mix of annoyance and contempt. "Follow me," he'd said slowly, grunting a little. Once his colossal frame had turned, Chris raised his eyebrows and smirked at the giant's back. For good measure, he stuck out his tongue in a rather childish gesture.

Old Charlie elbowed Chris in the ribs and put his index finger to his lips, mouthing a "shhh." Chris might not be intimidated by Braydon but Charlie sure was.

The hulking brute must have stood over six-foot-six. His muscles, bulging beneath the oversized pin-striped business suit, reminded Chris of Tina over at the Boar's Head. Of course, physical size was their only similarity. Tina was open and friendly and would never be caught dead in a monkey suit like the one worn by the Neanderthal walking ahead of them. *I'll bet the two of them would have one heck of a rumble,* Chris thought. *I'd pay money to see that fight.*

But his attention quickly turned away from their ungracious host. Chris stared with awe as he entered the great hall. He could only stand motionless. His neck jerked upward, jaw dropping open, as his eyes were drawn to the ceiling three stories above, where gigantic cedar joists held up the roof. Slowly his head returned to ground level, taking in all of the details on the way down.

It was really an indoor courtyard, easily 50 feet wide and almost 100 feet long. Chris had never seen anything like it in his life. He'd scarcely been able to imagine anything like it could exist.

"Wait here," Braydon grumbled, holding one great palm outward. He then lumbered off, disappearing into a doorway.

Gazing around the room once again, Chris noted balconies along the interior walls, indicating each of the two floors above. Ornate french doors could just barely be seen behind thick red and black plaid flannel curtains. Apparently each room had its own indoor balcony to match the ones on the outside of the lodge.

The wide french doors on the lakeside wall were flanked by a beautiful double staircase rising to the second floor. Railings carved from knurled and knobbed trees led the way. These two sets of log stairs angled and then met over the center doors.

Four large skylights allowed the bright, warm afternoon sun to shine against the eastern wall, providing the space with the feel of the outdoors. The floor below was comprised of uneven square stepping stones, each complete with faux jagged edges set into concrete. The concrete between each stone, a quarter inch below, was embedded with sand to complete the outdoor feel.

However, when Chris bent down to feel the edges, they were anything but rough. *Only looks that way for the guests*, he thought. *But no accidents here.*

Two massive stone fireplaces stood stolidly opposite each other on the north and south walls. The opening for each firebox was about five feet tall and probably double that in width. Of course, both fireplaces here were cold and lonely during the summer days. While one fireplace was along the exterior wall, the other was actually a pass through into the cavernous, professional kitchen, creating a window to the stainless steel prep tables and appliances beyond. When he was young, Chris had once read a storybook about medieval knights and castles. One drawing in the book showed such a massive fireplace, where whole pigs could be slowly roasted, or entire trees could be burned during yuletide banquets. *I'm sure our whole cabin could have roasted marshmallows around one of those*, he thought.

Lush furniture sat in intimate groupings throughout the hall. Some included luxurious couches and love seats, obviously plushy and comfortable, arranged around small, round coffee tables. At other spots, cushioned chairs surrounded round tables. The furniture was made using a thick, darkly stained, rustic-looking wood.

Built-in glass display cases covered most of the walls on the ground level. Even from a distance, small interior lights illuminated the variety of native artifacts housed within.

All in all, the hall had a homely feel. On first glace, the furnishings could have belonged in any home in northern Michigan, with the exception of the sheer amount of space. Chris, however, knew better. These were one-of-a-kind pieces, and though they had the look of the everyday, they were all of the highest quality and price.

Probably the greatest treasure in the lodge's massive hall was the chandelier. Hanging directly in the center of the room about 15 feet above the floor by three thick cables, it was a piece of art itself, as much a tribute to beauty as it was to function. The chandelier was composed of five parallel wooden rings, each created to resemble gigantic wagon wheels. These were stacked one above each other, the widest in the middle, creating a globe-like configuration. Each ring was ornately carved and held a series of yellow-tinted light bulbs shaped like candle flames. However, the most striking aspect of this truly amazing chandelier was the antlers. The entire structure was covered with sharp, pointed antlers, each set bleached a pure white. Some were wide and gigantic, while others had many tines. These antlers crisscrossed and wove through and among each other, creating an elaborate framework for the glowing bulbs to diffuse light all over the lodge. It was all very stunning.

Chris could only stand and stare at the chandelier, wondering at the inestimable time and money it took to create such a fabulous piece of art.

If the outside of the lodge was impressive, this enormous interior space was certainly a testament to the luxuries that money could buy. It was a place affordable to only the richest and most powerful.

Old Charlie didn't need to say anything. He just watched and smiled as the young man took it all in.

Suddenly, Braydon was standing right over the two guests. Both of them jumped, surprised that the big man could have sneaked up on them so stealthily. He held out a sealed manila envelope. It looked rather small in his giant paw of a hand.

"Here you go. If you'll excuse me, I have business to attend to." He squinted his eyes and gave the two men a menacing look. "You may look for one minute longer and then you must go." Though it sounded funny that way, in a sort of edgy, Eastern European accent, Chris was pretty sure Braydon had meant every word. They'd have exactly one minute.

Once the big man had squeezed himself back through the door from whence he had come, Chris and Charlie both breathed easily. Champ had sent the two of them to simply pick up a package from Mr. Wellington. Now that their errand was complete, Chris knew they needed to get going. However, he was drawn by the lighted display cases. He cautiously strode over to the nearest wall and followed the glass cases. Inside were elaborate headdresses, chipped weapons and tools, jewelry and beadwork.

"This is a museum-quality collection, man," Chris said in wonderment, checking out the display placards on each piece. "Ottawa, Ojibwa, Potawatomi." In the third case, one word caught the young man's attention. "Omeena," he whispered slowly, remembering back to the story his aunt told only a few days earlier.

"We really should get goin' now, you know," Charlie said nervously, looking around the room, expecting Braydon to show up again at any moment.

And then Chris's attention was drawn to a particular piece. "Wait, a minute," he said pointing toward one glass shelf of artifacts. "Look at this, Charlie. That's Aunt Natalie's necklace," Chris said, surprised. "I'm sure of it. See, it has the four black gemstones."

Charlie tried to laugh, but it only came out rather muted, rather timid. "Maybe it's just a coincidence. Maybe this one only looks like the one your aunt had."

"No way," Chris declared. "This is hers, I'm sure of it. I remember it well, Charlie. I grew up seeing it every summer of my life. And now, somehow, Harris has gotten a hold of it."

"So how did it end up here?" Charlie asked, talking in a whisper. His head nervously began glancing around the room.

Chris thought for a moment. Then it all clicked. His eyes lit up in understanding. "The break-in at Aunt Natalie's this past winter. I'll bet Harris was behind it. He just had to have the necklace for his collection. That rotten old geezer," Chris growled under his breath. His hands were clenched in fists.

"Well, there's not much we can do about it now," Charlie said, trying to pull Chris away from the trophy case. "Tell your Aunt Natalie. She can handle it. We need to get going."

With that, they heard a door slam someplace deep inside the lodge. Heavy footsteps resounded on creaky floorboards. Both men looked at each other and nodded.

"Okay, but we'll be back," Chris stated, taking one final glance at the glass case that housed so many precious artifacts. Then he and Charlie scampered for the main doorway and the relative safety of the outdoors.

***

A single-file line of camp girls strolled down the forest path, oblivious to the world around them. They were singing the chorus of a camp song and had no idea they were being watched.

The kids were all wearing their official green uniforms embellished with the Green Lake Music Camp logo. But unlike their counselor, who sported a fancier green polo shirt, these midgets wore simple t-shirts. They all wore khaki shorts because of the intense heat that followed them like a curse all day and all night.

Their counselor looked just like a mother duck leading a line of ducklings.

The sun was already on its journey back to the horizon, and long shadows were creeping through the trees and underbrush. Somewhere high overhead, a whip-poor-will called out the refrain to its own song.

The watcher inched around a big oak tree and exclaimed, "Psst! Over here!"

The leader of the line whipped her head around, looking for the source of that voice, a voice that was so familiar. The line of girls stopped abruptly, their joyous song cut off.

"Psst!" Chris called again. "Hey, Linda, over here!"

Linda Hammond, the counselor at the head of the line, grinned in amazement at the half-hidden young man. This was indeed an unexpected surprise. She certainly didn't anticipate seeing him again so soon (or even at all). "How'd you get here?" she said, the corners of her mouth turning upward in a smile.

Leaning around the tree and pointing over at old Charlie's truck in the nearby parking lot, Chris said, "Hopped a ride in. I just had to see you again." He gave her another wide smile.

The midgets began giggling. Linda turned back and hushed them. Even under the shade of the thick canopy of leaves, Chris could see she was quickly turning a bright shade of red.

The young man sneaked out from behind the large oak and strolled over to the group of girls. "Hey there, pretty lady. Where are you taking these cute little girls on a gorgeous day like today?"

Linda flashed him a genuine smile, her eyes sparkling. She pointed toward the large central building 50 yards down the path. "We're on our way to a concert. You could join us if you wanted to."

"Normally, I'd love to, but I'm late for work at Aunt Natalie's. I just got time to ask you one question."

A little girl near the front of the line asked, "Is it a serious question?" This was followed by a whispering chorus that made its way up and down the line.

Chris gave the little girl a playful smirk and then bounced his eyebrows up and down. "It is indeed a serious question."

Again, the troupe of midgets giggled.

Turning back to Linda, Chris confidently asked, "Would you like to go out with me this Sunday night? There's a great bonfire a friend of mine is having. It would give us a chance to get to know each other a little better."

Linda gave him a knowing half smile, silently guessing as to the events that would occur at the bonfire. "I'm not a drinker, you know," she said, leaning in so the midgets wouldn't hear her.

"That's okay, I don't drink either," Chris answered softly. "Not my thing." He shook his head, then flashed a silly grin at her. "We can make fun of the guys who do. I'll make sure I bring a cooler of Cokes along. Will that work for you?"

She only had to think about it for half a second. "Alright, it sounds fun."

"Will you be done here at eight?"

"I'm sure I can get someone to cover for me for a few hours. I'll meet you out front by the camp sign. That way no one here can make fun of your truck."

Chris laughed. "It's really Charlie's truck. But don't worry, I'll have something better to pick you up in."

Linda looked up at him, a sense of wonderment flooding her otherwise sensible mind. "I'll see you then."

Nodding politely and giving her a quick, silly (and utterly pretentious) bow, the young man skipped up the hillside and made his way to Charlie's truck. Linda and the girls all waved at him before he slipped back into the passenger side.

"Miss Linda, he sure is cute," one little freckle-faced girl teased.

"Is he gonna marry you?" another girl asked.

Linda only stared at the girls with an open-mouthed grin. *You little brats*, she thought as the whole line began giggling again. But in a few seconds, she joined them, her blush already fading.

***

In the deep darkness of the Michigan night, the truck sped up Betsie River Road. Though the driver could feel the jarring from every rut and stone that protruded through the hard-packed country road, the pickup's passenger had lost most of his senses an hour or so earlier.

Somewhere overhead, pushing its way past the puffy night clouds, the moon had begun to illuminate the world in its silvery glow.

"Gawd, it's hot out here," Gerald slurred from the passenger side of the cab. His hands fumbled with the window crank.

"Don't you dare put that window down," Mildred hollered back at him. "I don't need the wind blowin' the curlers outta my hair."

The passenger window moved down a few inches before Gerald's hands lost their faculties. The old lady swore several oaths before she realized he wasn't listening to her.

Her husband was passed out cold, his head vibrating against the glass.

"You old fool," Mildred growled at him. "Call me to pick you up at two in the morning 'cause you can't drive home. So I gotta drive all the way out here just so as I can drag yer pimpled butt outta the bar." Then she yelled at him, "And you aren't even listening!"

From the bench seat she grabbed today's *Record-Eagle*, still rubber-banded together, and threw it at her husband. She'd have really whacked him with it if he hadn't been leaning up against his door and just out of reach. As it was, the rolled-up newspaper bounced off of Gerald's John Deere cap, knocking it to the floor.

Gerald began mumbling, and after a few seconds, coherent words emerged. "Gotta go, pull over Milly. Gotta go."

"Can't you hold it?" she shot back.

"Nope." Just that one word answer.

She sighed deeply and dramatically, though Gerald was far too gone to appreciate it. Then Mildred's eyes narrowed to slits and she looked over at him slyly. She hit the brakes far harder than was necessary. Her slight body caught on the lap belt, restraining her behind the wheel. However, Gerald wasn't wearing his belt. He slid forward on the saddle blanket that covered the weathered and beaten-up bench seat and rammed his forehead onto the dashboard. "Ow!" he yelled, somewhere between confusion and anger, his hands coming up to rub the bump that was quickly rising. "Whaddaya do that fer?"

"You get what you deserve, you old goat," Mildred shot back at him. A few moments of silence went by before she realized he wasn't moving. "Well, get after it. Go on, now."

Her husband of 48 years had no more success with the door handle than he had with the window crank. With no luck there, he tried to batter his way out, shoving his shoulder against the passenger door. Obviously, that wasn't working either.

Exasperated, she asked no one in particular, "Oh, God, do I gotta do everything for you?" She threw the '67 Ford pickup in park and climbed out. Already the road dust had caught up to them, and now it swirled in the headlights. Mildred coughed, waving her hands in front of her to disperse the dust as she stomped around the front end and over to Gerald's side.

His body nearly wiped her out as he poured out of the truck's passenger door. It was a miracle that Gerald's work boots stayed on when he hit the road, since the laces were untied and the tongue was flapping down. His knees did buckle a bit, but he managed to right himself on the door. With Mildred to guide him (she pinched his elbow until he yelped), he made it the few steps to the slight embankment on the road's side.

Her arms crossed in front of her chest, Mildred waited for her husband to relieve himself. After a few seconds, she began tapping her shoes on the dirt road impatiently.

And then, as if there had been some great wind blowing down from West Grand Traverse Bay, the old man started reeling. Of course, there was no wind this evening, and that made what happened next all the more hilarious. One of Gerald's hands was still trying to help him urinate, but the other began wildly swinging in the night air. It was a futile attempt at regaining balance. His body made a few circular gyrations before all was lost. A second later, like the toppling of a mighty tree in the woods, Gerald fell to the soft soil at the roadside.

If she hadn't been so angry at him already, Mildred probably would have cracked up laughing. As it was, she could only stare at him, exhaling in a deep, growling grunt. *Just figures*, she thought.

Disgusted, she shrugged her shoulders to heaven. "I give up. I can't take anymore!" Then she turned back to her husband. He was still lying in the ferns. "Fine! Stay there! Stay there all night!" She kicked the passenger door and it slammed shut. Gerald didn't move an inch from his location.

Still grumbling, she climbed back in the truck and yanked down on the gearshift. Her foot slammed on the gas and the pickup tore off down the dirt road, fishtailing a bit and kicking up gravel and dust all over the prone man.

In a few minutes, the dust settled back to the ground. Now that the pickup's engine faded away, the night was eerily silent.

Raising his sleepy head, the old man looked around, disoriented. "Where ya at, Milly?" he asked the darkness around him. "Where'd ya go?"

For a few seconds, there was no noise in the north woods to answer him, save the mosquitoes that had begun buzzing around his hairy ears. And then, an answer did come, though it wasn't from his wife. A deep, throaty growl, lasting a good 10 seconds, echoed through the woods around him. It seemed to come from everywhere and from nowhere at all.

Gerald sobered immediately. He suddenly found himself standing upright and looking off down the road. The moon, though not quite clearing the treetops, still cast enough light down so the old timer could distinguish the road from the forest beyond. His eyes darted in all directions, his head swiveling in nervous jerks back and forth.

The growl rolled past him a second time, and this time Gerald sensed that it came from down the road. As he looked back that way, he glimpsed at a pair of little yellow lights off in the distance. They were very bright, almost like little golden globes suspended in midair. But his breathing stopped when he saw them blink, twice. They weren't lights—they were eyes!

He didn't think, he only reacted. Summoning every ounce of strength left in his intoxicated body, Gerald bolted down the road, looking like a newborn fawn who was still learning to use its legs.

He'd forgotten to zip his pants, and within a few seconds he ran right out of his unlaced boots, tripping only a little. But he hardly noticed, even as his socks flapped on the dirt road. He was only thinking he had to keep moving, keep running, as far from that sound as he could get.

There was no one here to help him, no one to rescue him way out here in the woods.

For a third time, the growl reverberated in the darkness. The old man was sure his time was up.

And at that moment, Gerald saw a pinpoint of light on the road ahead. Salvation! He broke into a run, the fastest his wobbly legs would take him.

The light split in two and became a pair of headlights. Still, Gerald kept running forward, never looking back.

But the headlights were coming far too quickly. There was no time to jump out of the way. He'd only replaced one danger with another.

Gerald put his hands up over his face as the vehicle screeched to a halt barely three feet in front of him. For the second time in the evening, road dust blasted by the old man, covering his clothing and skin in fine gray powder.

Through the swirling dust, he could see his wife behind the steering wheel. But there was no time to explain, no time to thank the stars for saving his life this time. There wasn't even time to open the door.

Rather than fight with the door handle, Gerald took another step along the truck and then nimbly leapt into the truck's bed. It was an extraordinary feat for someone of his age and current inebriated condition. But he slipped over nonetheless, landing on the myriad of loose items covering the bed.

"Floor it, Milly!" he shouted, his head ringing and bleeding from being nicked by an old cement block.

Mildred couldn't figure out what her husband was so upset over until she saw the creature standing in the road about 80 feet ahead in the glow of the headlights. It was slightly crouched, its knees bent and paws spread, ready to attack. Its shoulders were hunched, and its clawed hands opened and closed rhythmically from the long, dangling, hairy arms. In her mind, Mildred could hear the clicking as its claws scraped each other in anticipation.

That was enough for her. Her arms weren't strong enough to turn the truck's big steering wheel around in such tight quarters. Instead, she gunned it straight toward the creature.

The Ford's big V8 roared, the back tires kicking up stones in all directions. It wouldn't reach full speed in such a short distance, but the vehicle still became a heavy-duty battering ram.

Mildred gripped the wheel with both hands, her knuckles already turning white. The truck closed the distance in only a few seconds. The creature didn't budge, it only continued to clench and open its clawed hands, eyes glowing evilly back at her.

The last Mildred saw of the beast was its horrific smile, its teeth glistening in the headlights. Then it sprang off its crouched legs, nimbly leaping straight up in the air just before the inevitable impact would have occurred.

Gerald, now rolled onto his back, watched as the hairy beast catapulted up over the truck's cab and somersaulted in midair. He could see it fairly well between the glow of the headlights ahead and the moon above. The creature completed two full flips before landing flat-footed at the far end of the truck's bed. It turned around to face the man lying before it.

His mouth now open in shock and horror, Gerald tried to scream but nothing came out.

Mildred felt the impact of the creature's landing and began swerving the truck back and forth wildly down the road. The monster's balance was upset immediately and it groped its clawed hands downward to find the top edge of the tailgate.

Wasting no time, Gerald's hands grabbed anything they could find and threw it at the beast. First was the L-shaped lug wrench, then two beer bottles, and then his hands gripped the car jack. There wasn't much room to really wind up, but Gerald pulled his hands to the front of the bed (he only noticed later that his right hand was scraped up pretty badly by that same cement block that had earlier lacerated the side of his head) and heaved it with all of his might.

It was an opportune moment. The creature was still trying to find the tailgate with one claw while defending itself with the other. And while attempting to balance, its feet were slipping on a number of old, rusty bolts that were rolling around. The car jack caught the beast right at the top of its chest, just below the neck. There was a thud and an audible "whoof" as air left the creature's lungs. And then the monster toppled backwards, its knees bending over the tailgate. Another thud sounded as some part of its anatomy bounced off the bumper, and then it was gone from sight.

Mildred had no interest in stopping to see what it was. She had no interest in heading back toward home, not this night, no sir. She sped off down the road. Before she realized it, they'd gone right through the village of Karlin and on to M-115, heading for Mesick.

CHAPTER 6
Ambush

"Come on in, Chris," Champ said smiling. "Grab a seat, son."

The young man plopped down on the metal folding chair opposite Champ's desk. He removed his ball cap and was nervously squeezing it in his hands. Ordinarily, camp staff evaluations were no big deal. However, Chris had a nagging feeling that something was up. Champ had seemed distant in the previous few days, like he was daydreaming, staring off into the woods or the lake or just looking at seemingly nothing with some sort of nostalgia. And usually Chris's evaluation was the first of the bunch, since it was always easiest to begin with the best ones and work downward.

The older man shuffled a few papers around on his large desk. Finally finding the papers he wanted, he gave one copy to Chris while reading from the other.

"Of course, your evaluation is stellar as usual. You and I both know that." He annoyingly tapped the eraser tip of his pencil on the desk pad while Chris looked over the paperwork. When the young man's eyes looked up, Champ said slowly, "Now for the bad news. You know times are tough. And we've had it pretty bad the last few years." The camp director exhaled deeply. "I'll tell it to you straight, son. Fact is, we can't keep open for another season."

Startled, Chris could only stare back at his boss in bewilderment. That wasn't what he expected at all.

"I know it's a shock, and I know that camp has meant a lot to you over the years. And you have meant a lot to me, too. You're like the son I never had, you know. You're the best right-hand man anyone could ever ask for. But every season has to come to an end."

Taking a deep breath, Champ continued, "We've been offered a very generous sum by the Tuscarora Club. They want to buy us out.

"That errand I sent you and Charlie on the other day? To the Tuscarora Lodge? That packet had the paperwork for the transferring of the deed."

Chris felt sick. He'd played a part in the camp's demise without even knowing it.

"You know we've been selling chunks of the camp to them over the past couple of years. And things just aren't getting better around here. That fire last year wiped out four cabins and there's no way we can replace 'em. We just aren't getting enough money in anymore."

"You mean old man Harris is bullying you to sell?" Chris said angrily.

Champ shrugged his shoulders. "We've just been hit with bad luck over the past few years."

"Do you think it might be more than bad luck?" asked the young counselor. "Do you suppose that maybe someone has been changing our luck around here? Like old man Harris for instance?"

The camp director just looked back at his best worker, giving him a sigh. "Charlie's been bending your ears, too, huh? Yeah, I've heard all of his stories, his accusations. I have my suspicions, too, but we have no proof."

Wearily, Champ said, "I'm sorry, son, it's just the way things are. I wish it were different. Old Harris has me over a barrel. If I don't sell out to him, we'll end up losing the camp to the bank. Then I'm out with barely the shirt on my back. At least Harris is willing to pay at the average property value."

"It's not right. It's not fair," Chris said, shaking his head back and forth. His lips were curled in against his tightly clenched teeth.

"I knew you'd take it the toughest of anyone," said Champ tenderly. "That's why your evaluation was the last one this year. I didn't even bother to tell any of the other kids. They'll just get a letter from me in a few months explaining it all. They'll get over it without much trouble. But I knew I had to tell you in person."

Chris nodded slowly, studying the floorboards, unable to look Champ in the eyes. It was too painful.

"I'd like you to stay on one last week, if you're interested. Nights, too. 'Course, you won't be able to work for your aunt as much, I'll need you round here, but it'll be for your same daily pay. I can probably even find some extra to throw in. There are a lot of details that need to be taken care of before we close up for this winter. For this last time." Champ trailed off, lost in thought as he looked out the dusty window.

Chris finally looked up and nodded to the aging camp director. He'd do anything for Champ. Aunt Natalie would understand.

He'd gladly put in the extra hours, not for the pay, but to take the burden off of his longtime friend and mentor. However, he still hated that it came down to this.

Chris thought he saw a tear drop in the corner of his old friend's eye.

***

Chris and Brett picked up Linda in the Plymouth Volare right at 8 outside the Music Camp. They hit the Dairy Queen first and had dinner. As the sun sank below the horizon and they headed south out of Interlochen, they chatted about that new Star Wars movie that had been such a hit all summer long. Chris was glad for anything to take his mind off of camp. The two boys were surprised at how much Linda had been into the movie. She, of course, was a big Han Solo fan.

They turned off on Penn Loch Colony Road south of the two lakes. The little subdivisions dwindled into a mix of farm lands and woods. The beautiful rainbow mix of colors in the sky had faded into a muted maroon and deep violet. They turned off down a dirt road called State Park Highway. Halfway down, they found the backwoods two-track leading out to Tina's bonfire. This trail was so insignificant that it didn't even warrant a road sign.

And yet, despite the complete isolation of the area, they did actually pass a car parked along the side of the road. It was a dark blue sedan, one of those older ones with the really long trunk. Though the others didn't seem to notice, Chris got a good glimpse at the driver who seemed really out of place here on a nearly deserted back road. He was sitting behind the wheel with the window glass fully raised up. *It has to be a hundred degrees in there*, Chris thought. And yet the driver was wearing a dark suit jacket over a white collared shirt, his tie still snugged up tightly despite the quickly approaching night. The only feature that stood out was the black sunglasses that hid most of his face.

Brett's Volare passed right by the parked sedan and turned up the two-track toward the party spot. A few moments later, Chris had forgotten all about it, anticipating this night with Linda. Normally, he could remember faces well, but this guy just slipped away with the last of the daylight, replaced in his mind by the beauty at his side.

They passed by a couple of ancient, dilapidated barns and abandoned houses that were crumbling back to the earth. It was rather spooky, like something out of a New England folktale or ghost story. If they weren't heading for a party, Linda wondered why anybody would ever come out this way.

Brett had to drop them off at the bonfire because, unlike them, he had a curfew. He also had a lot of chores to do even before the sun came up the next morning. He couldn't afford to be out late. But, since Chris didn't have a vehicle of his own up north, Brett was the knight in shining armor. The Volare might not have been gallant, but it was still better than borrowing either Charlie's Willys or Aunt Natalie's International. "You guys sure you'll be okay gettin' a ride home?" Brett asked.

Chris waved him off. "No problem, man. There's plenty of guys here that owe me one. We'll be fine. I'll see you later this week at Aunt Natalie's."

"Keep it real, man," Brett said, slapping his friend five. "You guys have a good time."

"See ya, dude," Chris responded, and the Volare spun around and tore off back down the two-track.

***

"What is this place?" Linda asked, partially fascinated, partially unnerved.

"They call it the old Penn Loch Colony," Chris answered. "It used to be some settlement from way back in the early 1900s, one of the first in this area. I don't know much about it other than it was deserted back in the 50s when Traverse City started really growing. Nobody really comes out this way anymore. I can't blame 'em."

Me either, Linda thought.

The bonfire wasn't huge, but it was warm and bright. They could see it through the encircling ring of cars and pickups. A few people were seated in lawn chairs around the fire while some were sitting on tailgates. Linda laughed at one pickup that was well equipped with a large patio umbrella in its bed, opened apparently to keep off the moonlight rather than the sunlight.

Chris had his little cooler in his left hand and he reached for Linda's hand with the other.

"Don't we need chairs?" Linda asked.

"Naw, we'll borrow a few from my good friend Mike. He always has a bunch in the back of his pickup just for such emergencies."

Walking into the circle of friends, Chris and Linda were hailed by most everyone in turn.

"Yo, Chris, how's it hangin'?" asked the first boy they encountered. "Who's the bunny, man?"

"Guys, this is my good friend Linda. Now, keep yer fingers off, dudes, she's with me." Chris slipped one arm around Linda's waist. Linda gave them all a polite wave and a shy smile.

Chris started naming off everyone seated around the fire. "This is my bro, Mike Antoine."

"I'd get up but I ain't in much condition to stand right now," Mike slurred, a wide, goofy smile stretching from ear to ear. He was lounging beneath the patio umbrella, a drink in one hand.

Continuing on, Chris pointed to several people who either waved or nodded back. "Those two over there are Sara and Sarah, and then you got Wayne, Artman, Josh, Mike the Miracle Man, Little David."

Little David did stand up and raised his can in a salute to Linda, though his head and shoulders barely cleared the tailgate of Mike Antoine's truck. "Hi, there," he squeaked in his alien voice.

"Wow, honey," Artman said. "That's impressive. Little David hardly says anything to anybody."

Wayne agreed, winking at Linda. "I didn't even know he spoke English. He must like you."

"And, hey, where's Barney?" Chris asked. "Isn't he here yet?"

"Barney's such a doofus," answered the Sara without the "h." She was braiding the other Sarah's hair into a twin pair of long ponytails. She giggled. "Last I seen him, he was dancing around with a broom."

"Yeah, I think he's spoonin' with it now," Miracle Mike said. "I'm pretty sure he's passed out in Josh's backseat already. He's a lightweight, you know."

Everybody broke out laughing.

"That guy over there is Zack. Watch out for him, he's a little strange." Chris dropped off to a whisper. Linda wasn't sure what that meant, but she was positive it wasn't very good. She was going to stick close to her date anyway. She smiled at that thought, of Chris being her date for the evening. They might only be at a bonfire, but it was still a first date.

"There's a few here I don't know," Chris also whispered. "And there's a few faces I do recognize but don't know their names. Anyway, you've met the important folks here. Except one."

Finally Chris brought Linda around the fire to meet the big feller. "And this is my man, Tina."

"Backatcha, man," Tina said, high fiving Chris.

"He's the bartender at the Boar's Head."

The big guy gently shook Linda's hand, which completely disappeared in his gigantic paws. "It is my pleasure to meet such a fine fox as you, little darlin'." He gave her a wink and a huge smile beneath his bushy beard.

"What are you guys jiving about?" Chris asked. Mike handed down a pair of lawn chairs, and Chris and Linda pulled them up to the fire near the others. The little cooler was opened, and Chris handed Linda a soda.

"We was just sittin' around talkin' music, you know?" Wayne said, leaning back in his folding chair.

"What's that new band you're always talkin' 'bout, Chris?" Tina asked. "ABCD or somethin' like that?"

"AC/DC," Chris responded, slowly emphasizing each letter. "They're gettin' a lot of air time on WTAC down where I'm from."

"Yeah, I heard of 'em," Miracle Mike said, rolling his eyes. "I'm tellin' ya, they ain't goin' anywhere. No one in the U.S. is gonna take to a bunch of chumps from Australia."

"You just wait," Chris argued. "I got the lowdown, man. They're coming to the Capitol Theater in Flint this fall, and I'm definitely goin'. You watch. They're gonna be big." He took a long sip of his soda.

"It'll be hard to ever top Aerosmith, dude," Tina said righteously. "They got my vote."

Both Sara and Sarah agreed immediately. Simultaneously, they both said "Steven Tyler," and everyone laughed again.

Artman shook his head. "No, no, no, the Stones, man."

Someone piped up from the other side of the fire, one fist held high. "Skynyrd, dude! Long live the Free Bird!"

The conversation turned ugly, with several slurs and insults thrown in. Even a few cans, mostly empties, went soaring across the fire.

Chris leaned over to Linda and whispered, "You wanna take a walk, get away from the crowd for a bit?"

"That would be nice," she whispered back. "I don't know if I can handle full contact rock and roll discussions."

Dodging another can, Chris stood and addressed the crowd. "Guys, as much as this conversation is stimulating our brains, we're in need of a little exercise. If you'll excuse us, gents, we're gonna hike out for bit to check out the local scenery."

"Later, skater," Tina said as the two walked off into the darkening field toward the old barns.

Wayne took a sip from his can, and then wiped his mouth with his forearm. "That boy's a real Casanova. I taught him everything he knows, you know?"

Miracle Mike sighed loudly and rolled his eyes.

As they left the circle of light, Chris and Linda heard someone behind them exclaim, "Man, who cut the cheese?" followed by an uproar of laughter.

***

Leaving the bonfire well behind, the young couple walked off through the wide expanse of pasture toward the old barns. It was still very warm out, and there was only a slight breeze that brushed the long grasses softly against their legs.

Chris reached over and slipped his hand into hers.

"You don't mind, do you?" Chris asked politely. He could see her smile in the last of the fading light.

"No, it's kinda nice, actually."

They passed one old barn, its weathered gray boards split and cracked. It looked like a strong wind could level the place pretty easily. *A little creepy, a little romantic*, Linda thought. Chris was staring off into the distance, lost in his own thoughts.

"You seem rather distracted. What gives?" she asked.

"Oh, just before I saw you at Green Lake the other day, Charlie and me were out at the Tuscarora Club. It was a rough afternoon. It's still eatin' me up inside."

"Why, what happened?"

Chris told her about Camp Doubennet closing and selling out to Harris Wellington. He also told her about Charlie's outlandish (and yet plausible) claims.

"Wow," she whispered. "That's really wild."

"That's not all," Chris said. "When we were inside the lodge, I saw my Aunt Natalie's special necklace in one of those display cases. You know, the ones with all of the Indian artifacts? You see, her house was broken into this past winter. The whole place was trashed. The only thing that was taken was this old Indian necklace she had that she kept up on the mantle in the living room. I don't think it was worth much, other than it was historic and a family heirloom and all. She wouldn't even let us kids touch it."

"What does it look like?" Linda asked. She'd dusted those cabinets and their contents once each week all summer long.

"It wasn't anything special looking. It was just a leather string with four shiny, black jewels that were long and looked like sharp claws or something. We kids used to joke that they were real claws from a saber-toothed tiger."

Astonished, Linda looked up at Chris. Excitedly, she said, "I know that piece. I know right where it is. I always thought it was a bit creepy, like it really didn't belong with everything else."

"Yeah, it kinda gives off its own vibe, you know? I know that seems weird, but it's true."

"And you're sure it's your aunt's?"

"Positive. I'll bet the old tycoon found out she had it and he wanted it for his collection."

Nodding her head, Linda agreed. "You may be right. I overhead Mr. Wellington talking to a group of visitors once, bragging that he had the finest and most complete collection of native artifacts from the Grand Traverse region."

"After what Charlie told me about how Harris has been 'acquiring' property to add to his club, it wouldn't surprise me a bit that he managed to 'acquire' Aunt Natalie's necklace."

"You know," Linda said slyly, "I work over there tomorrow. I've seen where Braydon keeps the keys to those cases. I could probably snag a hold of that necklace without much trouble."

"No, don't do that," Chris said alarmed. "I don't want you getting in trouble over this. I'll just let my aunt know. She can handle it. You don't know her, but she's pretty tough."

"Okay, if you say so," Linda said, quietly, looking away.

He could read the slightly mischievous look in her eyes and face.

"Really, don't do it. The less you have to do with that old coot, the better. He's a bad man, you know? A really bad man."

Chris stared off into the night in silence. He kicked a rock off into the darkness. "Sometimes I wish I did drink," he admitted. "Maybe that would help me forget all about camp and Harris and everything. Things just seem so stressed out right now. Normally, summer at camp is the best. I don't have to worry about home and family and school and all that. I get to get away from it all, you know?"

She knew the story already. It was her story all over again.

"And now it's all gone crazy. The camp's closing, Aunt Natalie's necklace's been stolen, and it all comes back to Harris and the Tuscarora Club. And yet I was the one who brought back the papers to sign over the camp. If I'd know what was in that packet, I'd have shredded it."

Linda looked up at him, a bit of the moonlight reflecting off her otherwise dark eyes. "Those things aren't your fault. You had no idea what you were picking up at the lodge. Besides, drinking wouldn't solve anything, you know? Those problems would still be there when you sobered up."

"Yeah, I know." Chris smiled again, looking deeply into her eyes. He momentarily put everything on the back burner. "At least with you here, things are certainly looking up."

Now that they were out behind the nearest barn, they could see the tiny pinpricks of stars emerging from the deep, velvety violet of the sky. As soon as they saw one, another came into view not too far away. The half disk of bright, silvery moonlight was just beginning to poke its way above the top edge of the forest beyond the pasture.

Chris pulled her directly in front of him. She was nearly a head shorter than him. His hands casually reached around her thin frame and his fingers met at the small of her back. He leaned down and in, their faces inching closer and closer together.

Linda reached her head upwards and closed her eyes. It was the perfect moment in the perfect setting.

But just before their lips could meet, a savage roar split the silence of the night, echoing through the nearby barn and rolling across the field.

Linda jumped, her body pressed right up against Chris's. Her arms instinctively wrapped around his waist. They looked over across the pasture and saw something staring back at them, about halfway to the forest beyond, maybe 50 yards away.

Even in the near darkness, they could see the animal's black shape. It looked like a gigantic wolf, panting and staring at them with glowing yellow eyes.

"Don't move," whispered Chris. "Just see what it does. More than likely it'll just head on its way."

The animal's head cocked to one side and then the other, as if listening to them. Still, it stared them down.

Since it wasn't moving, Chris summoned all of his bravery and shouted at it. "Go on, get!"

The black animal growled menacingly at them, its fangs reflecting the moonlight. Then it stood upright and looked down toward them. It must have stood seven feet or higher. A second later, it actually began walking toward them, its finger claws clicking together and making irritating scratching sounds, like someone running their fingernails on a chalkboard.

Horror filled the two young people. This was no mere animal. It was something much, much worse. Chris had momentary flashbacks to his youth. He'd grown up watching the many werewolf movies produced by Hammer Films on the Saturday night late show. But this was no Hollywood movie monster. This was no trick of special effects. This thing was real, and it was right here, stalking them.

Linda screamed, and the monster returned another thunderous roar, taking another step in their direction. It certainly had no problem balancing or walking upright.

What choice did they have? They couldn't stay where they were, with the monster closing in on them one step at a time. So Chris grabbed Linda's hand and the two bolted back toward the bonfire a couple of hundred yards away. From this distance, it looked very small indeed, just a flickering light in the darkness.

"In here!" Chris yelled, dragging Linda toward the old barn's open doorway. The two raced inside the dilapidated old building.

But the monster was too fast for them. It reached the doorway just seconds later. Chris knew they couldn't outrace it, but something caught his eye as they ran. Though it was nearly dark, he could still see the outlines of objects in the old barn. He pushed Linda into a side stall and grabbed hold of a pitchfork, standing guard in front of her.

Linda was sobbing. But despite her fear and panic, she tried her best to peer around Chris's shoulder without causing interference.

The beast slowly closed the gap, one menacing step at a time. Its eyes glowed a nasty, evil golden color, and its mouth turned up in a fang-filled grin. Chris wrinkled his nose and lip in disgust.

"What are you?" he yelled at the beast, but there was no reply other than a low, deep grunting that actually sounded like some hellish laughter.

Two seconds later, the creature was within striking distance. Chris lashed out at it with the pitchfork, but the move was of little use. In one easy swing of its clawed hand, the beast swiped away the weapon, sending it flying across the barn.

There was no escape. Protectively, Chris stepped in front of the girl and puffed his chest outward. His hands were clenched in fists at his sides. Linda buried her face in Chris's flannel shirt, tears pouring down her cheeks.

And suddenly, Tina was there. His massive frame seemed to fill the wide doorway. There was no thought on his part, only action.

Like a raging bull, the big man charged across the straw-covered barn floor. His quick action caught the beast off guard. It turned its attention from the couple and its glowing eyes opened wide in surprise.

In a move that would make any defensive end jealous, Tina lowered his shoulders and blasted right into the creature. Muscular, beefy arms wrapped around the monster's hairy midsection and Tina's solid shoulder drove right into its belly.

Air blasted from its lungs, the beast was too stunned to fight back. Its eyes bulged from their sockets and its muzzle hung open, gasping for breath.

Tina's momentum drove the two of them onward for another 15 feet until they made contact with one of the central support posts that held up the barn.

What happened next was inevitable.

The barn was well over a hundred years old, and its weathered exterior only gave an inkling of the true deterioration of its wooden structure. The support posts, once strong and stout, were on the verge of collapse. Coupled with the tremendous impact of the two massive beings, there was no way it could last.

Splinters flying in all directions, the post completely disintegrated.

A loud cracking and groaning of boards sliding and grinding against each other drew Chris and Linda's attention away from the battle. Debris began raining down.

With no time to lose, Chris grabbed Linda's hand and sprinted for the barn door, pulling her behind him. All around them, heavy beams and boards bounced off the floor.

Once outside, the two looked back just in time to see the entire structure collapse in upon itself. It reminded Chris of a house of cards he'd once seen a friend build only to have that friend's younger brother knock it down. Illuminated in the moonlight that now shined above the forest, the gambrel roof fell just before the walls folded inward. A great poof of dust and debris mushroomed up dozens of feet into the air.

"Tina!" Chris screamed into the night. "No!"

***

Within a minute, most of the people from the bonfire had arrived and surrounded Chris and Linda.

The dust settled; the night was still and quiet again. But neither Chris nor Linda could hear much after the loud crashing. Linda was still sobbing into Chris's flannel. Chris, meanwhile, was staring at the demolished barn in total disbelief. His good friend was gone, buried beneath the ancient structure. Tina had given his life to save them.

"I hear something," one person said.

"Maybe it's Tina!" another hollered back.

Indeed, there was a scraping sound of wooden boards being pushed aside. The group of kids held its collective breath, hoping against hope that their older friend would appear, that he'd be fine and joke about the whole thing.

A dark shape slowly pushed the debris to the side and climbed out of the wreckage. It shook itself off and stretched its limbs.

But it wasn't Tina who emerged from the rubble. Silhouetted against the rising moon, the creature stood upright, its back to them. It raised its arms up over its head; finger claws spread wide, it let loose a long, horrific howl directly at the silvery half orb in the sky.

The kids turned and bolted for their vehicles. The monster whipped around and curled its teeth up in rage. But it was slowed because its legs were still deeply entangled in the twisted jumble of boards. Once it freed itself, however, the race was on.

Out of breath, Chris, Linda, Artman, and Little David jumped up into Mike Antoine's truck bed. Wayne had pushed

Mike over to the passenger seat, knowing he was in no shape to be driving. The truck roared to life and a second later it tore off across the pasture. They were the last vehicle to leave the bonfire.

"Wayne, where are you goin'?" yelled Artman through the sliding pass-through window into the cab.

"I don't know!" Wayne hollered back from behind the steering wheel. "I'm just drivin', man!"

It was not a moment too soon. The creature came bounding into the firelight, its golden eyes blazing with the reflection of the fire. It turned its head one way and then another. Finally, with only one thing close enough to chase, it settled on Mike's truck.

Linda shrieked and pointed back from where they'd come. Chris swiveled his head around just in time to see the patio umbrella fly out the back. Little David had heaved it with all his might.

It wasn't much of a deterrent, though, because the creature leapt right over it in one well-timed bound.

The truck hit some sort of a large pothole or a slight ditch because everyone in the back felt an awful jerk down and then back upward. Dirt flew up over the hood and cab and sprayed everyone in the back. Two coolers went flying out of the bed, their contents spreading in all directions. A few folding lawn chairs followed suit. Chris would have slid right out, too, if it weren't for Artman grabbing his ankle at the last moment.

"Get the tailgate up!" Little David squealed in his high-pitched voice. "Or we're all going out that way!"

Chris inched his way toward the tailgate, but the rough road and the truck's swerving made it almost impossible to keep from tumbling out.

Linda could hardly watch, and yet she couldn't take her eyes off the scene that was unfolding before her. The young man she was falling in love with was bravely and selflessly trying to save them all. She poked Little David and pointed at Artman's straining muscles. The little guy knew what she wanted without needing to say the words. He nodded, and the two of them reached forward joining in the life-saving chain.

"Grab it, man," Artman wheezed between his clenched teeth. He was hanging onto Chris's legs with all his might while his own work boots were jammed in against the truck's side. Little David and Linda each had one arm around Artman and their other arms grasped the sidewalls of the pickup.

Of course, the truck was bouncing through the uneven field this entire time at top speed trying to evade their pursuer.

Fingers finally gripping the edge of the tailgate, Chris looked up just for a moment and saw the glowing golden eyes only a few feet behind. The rough terrain might be slowing down the truck but it had obviously not slowed the beast one bit. The creature would be in the truck with them in just a few seconds.

Tugging with all of his might, Chris raised the tailgate a few inches. "Pull me back!" he yelled. The human chain heaved backward, and Chris managed the lift the tailgate, slamming it back into locked position.

It was not a moment too soon. The beast was right behind the bumper, its jaws snapping, spittle flying in all directions. Its arms were pumping as it ran, just like a human sprinter. The finger claws reached outward with each arm movement, inching closer and closer.

"Man, you gotta kick it in!" Artman yelled through the sliding window.

Wayne yelled back, "I'm doing almost 45 here!" He knew he couldn't push the pickup much faster without facing a serious accident, what with all the holes, half-buried rocks, and ridges hidden by the tall grass. But he floored the gas pedal anyway at exactly the moment the truck encountered a slight embankment. Just as if they'd taken a well-practiced jump, the pickup took off airborne.

Every person in the back lifted nearly a foot off the truck bed. Several empty cans floated in midair, glistening in the moonlight, as did a miscellany of items like tie-down straps, bungee cords, and even a few pieces of firewood. Little David's legs actually went right up over his head.

And then the truck landed right on the two-track leading back to the State Park Highway. Everything in the back returned to the truck bed with a cacophony of rattling. Four bodies fell in a heap, with Artman grunting at the bottom of the pile. The vehicle careened side to side, tipping up onto its two left wheels at one point and nearly rolling over. But its wide wheel base eventually won out over its momentum, and Wayne gunned it down the two-track.

Now that they were on flat ground, the truck finally pulled away from its pursuer. Disengaging from the jumble of bodies, Chris sat up and looked back, watching as the glowing golden eyes slowly receded into the darkness behind them.

He exhaled deeply. The next thing he knew, Linda's arms were around his neck, squeezing him tightly.

CHAPTER 7
Alert

A unt Natalie?" Chris asked. "Have you ever been up to the Tuscarora Lodge?"

"No reason to," she replied, looking at him over her shoulder. "I've got no use for that rotten old Harris Wellington. He can burn in hell for all I care."

Chris nodded. *Why don't you tell me how you* really *feel?* he thought. Normally, she wasn't one to mince words, but Chris had never seen her quite this upset. He debated whether to tell her about the artifacts, since she was already obviously in a mood. After a few seconds, he decided this was as good a time as any.

"Um, Aunt Natalie?"

"Will ya just spit it out already?" she said, turning all the way around on her wooden swivel chair.

"You know I was out at the lodge the other day, and they got this huge collection of native artifacts."

Natalie looked back at Chris over the tops of her glasses, with both of her eyebrows raised and her lip curled. She looked like a librarian interrupted by a noisy school child.

"Well," Chris went on, "right in the middle in a huge display case, the biggest one in the room actually, I'm pretty sure I saw, well, your Indian necklace. Or at least, it looked a whole lot like that old necklace you always had on the mantle in the living room."

Natalie stared at her nephew without moving, without blinking.

"I'm sorry I brought it up," he said, taking a step back toward the office wall.

Natalie stood up and strode quickly over to her nephew. For a brief moment, Chris thought his aunt was going hit him or slap him or something. Despite her rough exterior and shrewd personality, he'd never known her to be actually violent in any way. However, she had a burning in her eyes that he'd never seen before. He had no clue what to expect.

Chris was already backed up against the countertop, so there was no place to escape. He steeled himself inside for whatever came next.

Natalie reached out both hands and grasped Chris's shoulders. She might not be a big lady, Chris thought, but her grip was like iron. He was expecting her to shout at him.

Instead she whispered, "You saw my necklace? Describe it to me, exactly as you saw it."

His eyes were locked with hers and they were only a foot apart. Chris stammered, "I'm pretty sure it was yours...it looked just like yours...there were the four claws, at least we always called them claws when we were little..."

"What color were they?" she demanded.

"That same shiny black," Chris answered quickly.

Natalie stared into his eyes for what seemed like an eternity. Then she loosened her grip and turned away, deep in thought.

Thirty seconds later, she looked back at her nephew. "Do you know what this means?"

Chris didn't answer, but he'd already had the same conclusion. Old Harris had stolen the necklace. Or he had someone steal it for him, more likely. Probably Braydon, his

Neanderthal assistant. Chris guessed that Harris's wheelchair probably wouldn't go up either the front or back stairs into Aunt Natalie's house very easily. But this also meant the old tycoon was the one responsible for trashing Natalie's house.

Oh, man, Chris thought, *she's going to hurt him. I really think she's going to go and actually hurt the old man.* By the time he looked up, she was already on her way to the door. She'd already traded her moccasins for her hiking boots.

"Where are you going?" Chris asked, though he was pretty sure he knew the answer already.

The fire still burning in her eyes, Natalie said slowly and forcibly, "I'm going to go get my property back."

Chris became a little excited seeing his aunt was ready to rumble. He wanted to see her blow her stack at that old tycoon. Chris already disliked Harris Wellington tremendously for how he treated the folks around Lake Ann, especially the staff at Camp Doubennet. Then add in his swindling of property from Champ and the pressure to sell the camp outright. And if he was the one responsible for the damages here, as well as stealing his aunt's property, Chris wanted to see him get what was coming to him.

"Can I go with you?" he asked cautiously, hoping to get in on the action.

"No, you stay here," she answered forcefully. Then her voice softened. "You don't need to get caught up in this, Chris. I do appreciate your offer, but this is something I need to take care of. Alone"

She headed for the door, only pausing to put on her wide-brimmed sun hat. Natalie looked back and gave him that warm, friendly smile he always loved. "I'll be back in a bit. Hold down the fort for me, okay?"

Chris had a weird thought. He wasn't sure exactly why it popped in his head. "What if you don't come back?"

Natalie gave a cough and a chuckle. "Mr. Wellington and I are going to have us a little chat, I think. It'll be a one-sided conversation, and it won't take long. And then I'm coming home with my property."

***

Linda sprayed cleaner on the wooden table and wiped it in wide circling patterns with her polishing cloth. She was only pretending to clean the Tuscarora Lodge's main room with any sort of gusto this evening. There were other thoughts on her mind, other plans for her last night working here for the old man.

Her eyes kept returning to the central display case at the room's far wall. Of course, she knew exactly what was behind that glass; she'd been purposely walking past it all evening. The upper third displayed a chieftain's headdress, its elaborate turquoise beadwork and long feathers hanging downward like the stingers on a jellyfish.

The bottom third of the case was taken up with three clay pots. These were a bit roughed up, showing some signs of aging and wear. Their once bright colors had faded, but you could still see the zigzagging patterns in blue, green, pink, and yellow.

But those two weren't important. It was the middle shelf to which her thoughts always returned. On a skin of bleached white fur, right in the middle of the shelf, was Chris's aunt's necklace. The four black, pointed gemstones stood out prominently against the soft, white background. *Chris was right*, she thought, looking at them on her first pass of the evening. *They do look like huge claws.* She'd even put her fingers up to the glass and imagined the comparison. Each gemstone was longer than any of her fingers. Anything with claws that big would be terrifying indeed.

The placard on the middle shelf proudly indicated that these were artifacts from the now defunct Omeena tribe.

Step one was complete. She'd scouted out the exact location of the necklace. Now she needed to reach it, to unlock the case.

Braydon kept basically all of the Tuscarora Club's keys, nicely labeled, on a large wall rack in his office. One key conveniently opened all of the display cases here on the first floor. She could see the beautifully stained deep cherry door to Braydon's office straight across from where she was now wiping down each of the large, wooden, high-backed chairs situated around the rectangular game table.

She'd begun to think of Braydon's office as the antechamber, the annex to Mr. Wellington's personal office beyond. *Beware, traveler,* she thought she'd read someplace, *for beyond this point there be dragons.* She'd been allowed to peer into Harris's inner office only one time, and that was plenty for her. Not only was it very dark, and rather spooky, but it was the one place in the entire lodge that smelled of age, like sweaty socks and medicines and snotty tissues that should have been thrown out months ago but have instead piled up and begun to rot. The remainder of the lodge was immaculate (thanks to the hired help like her), very clean and airy. Yet Harris's inner sanctum was a cave. Or maybe even a tomb.

It was like smelling death, she often thought. *I wonder if the old guy is dying?* Of course, he seemed rather decrepit and frail, only able to get around using his wheelchair. But he had a fire inside him; you could see that in his eyes and in his voice. His wits and intellect were sharper than a man half his age (or even younger).

The office suite was deserted now. Braydon had escorted Harris out a half hour ago. Most nights followed this same pattern. Around eight o'clock, these two would mysteriously leave the offices. Completely disappear was the better description. Linda had never seen them leave through the main hall; Harris's wheelchair made too many squeaks to miss. And having a basic idea of the lodge's floor plan in her head, Linda knew there weren't any doors to other sections of the ground floor from those offices. The long, dogleg-shaped kitchen bordered one wall and the other was the exterior wall facing the woods. There was no door to the outside there, only a large bay window that Harris kept closed and covered with heavy drapes.

Maybe he has a secret elevator in there, she mused. *Takes him directly upstairs to his penthouse suite. No muss, no fuss.* Actually, it didn't seem that far-fetched. A man with that much money could have anything he wanted built into this edifice. *Shoot, he could have two elevators in there if he wanted, one for him and one for Braydon.* Plus, there were no other bedrooms or guest rooms on the ground floor anyway.

More than a half hour had passed since she saw the line of light vanish from under the cherry door. It was a good sign.

Looking around the deserted hall, Linda made up her mind. Now was the time. She set her cleaning bottle and cloth on the table and tip-toed her way to the office door. Just to be safe, she quietly knocked before turning the handle. "Mr. Braydon? Mr. Harris?" she said cautiously. No answer. No light.

So, in she crept. Again, being cautious lest someone be in the inner office, she flipped on the switch and exhaled deeply, almost waiting to be caught. But there was nothing, nobody was around. The only sound was the ticking of the seconds on the clock on Braydon's desk. Linda looked to the wall knowing exactly where to find the key. *Right where I remember you,* she thought, slipping the little key fob off its hook and palming it in her right hand.

Creeping back out the door after flicking the light switch off, Linda stole her way across the great hall. It had never seemed that far before. Her eyes kept flitting from side to side, even up to the windows and balconies on the upper levels, looking for anything or anybody that would give her away. But there was still no one there. It was midweek in August, and that meant the lodge would be deserted. Guests wouldn't start arriving until Thursday.

It took what seemed like an eternity to cross the hall, weaving in and around the groupings of furniture, before she reached the display cases. Yet again, Linda peered all over the great room, her eyes studying the shadows in the recesses and corners, the reflections of the overhead lights on the windows and sliding doors. There was no movement. The lodge was lifeless.

Her right hand trembled a bit as it raised the key and fitted it into the little lock. The click seemed to echo through the main hall, and Linda flinched. After another pause, she opened the door which thankfully didn't squeak or make any sort of noise at all. And then, she was face to face with the necklace.

Behind the glass, it didn't seem like anything out of the ordinary. Sure, it was a unique piece, just as Chris described it.

Now, however, with her fingertips just touching the claw-shaped gemstones, Linda could almost feel a sort of power emanating from it. There was nothing she could exactly identify, but her senses had jumped into high alert. It was as if there was just the slightest of vibrations, like energy waves flowing from the black gemstones into her fingers and right up her arms. It was spooky, yet electrifying at the same time.

Her fingers made contact, and Linda jumped back. *Is it my imagination*, she thought, *or are those stones hot?* Her fingers cautiously stole forward again. She squinted her eyes to slits in anticipation. But this time there was no shock, no static charge, no heat, nothing. *Just a necklace, an old artifact.*

Whew! she breathed. *Got myself all worked up over nothing.*

Hands closing over the gemstones, Linda pulled the necklace out and carefully shut the glass door. *Now, where do I put this thing?* She didn't have any pockets that could conceal it, and she didn't bring a purse or bag with her when she worked. Looking at the necklace, she shrugged. *Guess I get to wear you home.*

Just before the necklace slipped down over her head, a thought ran through Linda's mind. *Should I really be doing this?*

And then the necklace slid fully over her hair, her face, and the tip of her chin, coming to rest just behind the collar of her green camp shirt. Linda could feel a distinct warmth transferring from the gemstones to her skin at the base of her neck. Again, she felt that sense of power and energy flowing into her body, but this time it was overwhelming. Her cheeks and forehead flushed as it rose upward, enveloping her brain.

Her eyes rolled upward behind their sockets and her head lolled backward.

***

Somewhere in the north woods darkness, a creature suddenly stood upright. Its eyes were closed tightly, but its other senses sharpened. Its pointed, canine ears twitched, reading the slightest vibrations that permeated the natural world around it. Rather loudly, the creature sniffed the air, its muzzle wrinkled up, displaying its razor-sharp fangs.

It had heard the call of the necklace, the *zemi,* many times since awakening more than two centuries before. And it had been tracking its stolen treasure ever since. The creature had already reclaimed several of the *itZic shileeteh,* its sacred "razor-claws," absorbing the powers of those black stones back into its supernatural body. Every razor-claw the creature recovered only increased its strength, its invincibility.

Two decades had passed since the creature had found the last black stone. Now it heard the *zemi* calling again. The signal wasn't as strong as it had been when all of the *itZic shileeteh* were originally together. They'd been separated over the past 270 years. Lost, even, perhaps.

Lost, that was, except to a creature with the ability to hunt them down. To reclaim what had been stolen.

In only a fraction of a second, the creature zeroed in on the *zemi's* signal. It was very clear, and there were likely several of the black gemstones together this time. Even though its eyes were closed, the creature's mind could see the trail to them as plain as day.

Wasting no time, the creature bounded away through the forest, making no sound whatsoever.

***

Linda awoke to find herself slumped down in the thick padding of a brown leather recliner. She blinked a few times and then rubbed her eyes with the heels of her hands. She couldn't believe what she was seeing.

The glass case from which she'd removed the necklace was on the far side of the great hall, nearly a hundred feet away! She had no recollection of how she'd traveled all the way across the room and passed out here in the chair. Linda's eyes were drawn to the huge mantle clock over the fireplace nearby. Almost a half hour had passed while she was sleeping. *Unconscious more like it*, she thought. The only thing she remembered was putting on the necklace. The rest had disappeared.

At that, her fingers instinctively rose to her neck, feeling for the four long, pointed gemstones. They were neither hot nor issuing any sort of energy, at least not any she could tell. They were just lifeless gemstones.

Linda used her thumbs to widen out the necklace thong a bit, tucking it fully beneath the collar of her shirt where it couldn't be seen.

Then, panic shot through her. Her unplanned nap had cost her valuable time. She'd be relying on Braydon to shuttle her back to the music camp, and he was due to check on her in just a few minutes.

It was strangely difficult to get up out of that comfortable leather recliner. Linda's body kept telling her to just sit, just relax, maybe even take another nice nap. But her mind was reeling, knowing she had to get that key back into Braydon's office before he got back. He probably wouldn't notice the missing necklace for some time, but he'd definitely notice an empty spot on the key rack.

Finally disengaging herself from the chair, Linda skittered to the office door. *Still dark inside*, she cheered to herself. *Still got time.*

In just a few seconds, the key was returned to its rightful spot on the wall. Linda breathed a deep sigh of relief.

Now, back outside before he returns, she began, but her eye was caught by something over across the room.

Now she was really torn. Part of her mind was screaming, *Get out, get away, you're gonna get caught!* Yet another part was far too curious. And she was in well over her head already anyway.

Her curiosity won out.

Spread out on Braydon's enormous desk was a USGS topographical map and a set of blueprints. The map displayed the immediate area adjacent to Lake Doubennet, including the Tuscarora Club property, the few homes in the area, and Camp Doubennet. There were big circles around each of the individual property owners labeled with dates, most of them in the upcoming months. The blueprints were for the expansion of the Club to include a golf course, another lodge, and a number of condominiums that all surrounded the lake. Camp Doubennet would be leveled, as would the other homes and cottages.

However, what caught her attention the most was a series of brightly colored binders. On the cover of one was a picture of a small oil derrick and the words "Niagara Reef: Northern Michigan Basin." On another was a nice picture of what appeared to be Lake Michigan and the title, "Middle Silurian Pinnacle Reef-Growth Models." She had no ideas what either of these two meant. But there were also fancy folders and official-looking documents from Shell Oil, Gulf Oil, Unocal 76, and British Petroleum, and these she did recognize.

Linda lifted the edge of the first USGS map and found a Grand Traverse County road map below. There were notes scribbled all over it in red marker. As she studied the writing for a few seconds, she realized the markings all over Grand Traverse County, as well as Kalkaska and Benzie counties, were sites for oil rigs. Dozens of oil rigs. She rolled the top map back into place. Sure enough, there were several potential drill sites in the land the Tuscarora Club either owned or wanted to acquire from the nearby residents.

Linda just stared at the desk and its spread of information.

What it all boiled down to was the overall plan showing the Tuscarora Club's complete conquest of the area. And according to the notes, it was being carried out with questionable means. None of these adjacent landowners would be selling out to the Club if they knew the real value of their property lay well below ground level.

If Champ at Camp Doubennet knew what he was sitting on, he'd destroy that deed transfer in a heartbeat.

She had to tell someone about all of this.

But who would believe her? It would be her word against the word of Harris and Braydon.

Then it hit her. Evidence—I need evidence. And the means of obtaining that evidence became apparent immediately. Situated atop a nearby bookshelf was a Polaroid instant camera – one of the newer, expensive SX-70 models. She knew exactly how to use it because they had one at Green Lake Music Camp. They used it to take pictures of the campers and then send these cheesy mementos home inside a card that read, *I Survived Green Lake Music Camp.* Parents loved them; the campers were mostly indifferent.

For the umpteenth time, Linda looked around for someone spying on her. Since the coast was still clear, she snuck across the wooden floor and grabbed the camera. After flipping it open, she stared at the folders, documents, and maps through the viewfinder. Not waiting another second, she began shooting. She took six photos and only after emptying the film pack did she panic. *He'll know all of the film's gone*, she thought.

Having frantically laid the necklace, the camera, and the six photos down on Braydon's desk, Linda searched the room for an additional film pack. She tried the cupboards, the drawers, and the various storage nooks. But nothing showed up. Now she was really panicking. She tried the closet. Bingo! Inside was a set of shelving that housed all sorts of paper products, office supplies, and on the very bottom shelf, she saw an entire box load of Polaroid instant Integral Film packs.

Kneeling down, Linda pulled the box out and removed a film pack. Then she quickly rose and turned back to the camera.

Her surprise was evident as she came face to face with Braydon. Well, her face was really only at his chest level. But she still jumped half a foot in the air and nearly fell backward into the closet's supply shelves. Her heart immediately went into overdrive as a sweat broke out on her forehead. She was sure she was blushing, too, since her ears were now red hot.

The big man looked from Linda to his desk and all of the Polaroid pictures that had finished their development. He frowned and shook his head. When he looked back at her with his emotionless, cold blue eyes, he also noticed the necklace protruding from beneath her collar.

"Mr. Braydon, I can explain," Linda started saying.

The last thing the girl saw was Braydon's beefy arm flying in her direction. Once his fist made contact with the side of her head, she felt only the briefest pain as she was knocked out cold.

***

Chris looked up again at the clock over his aunt's desk. It was almost nine o'clock, and Natalie had been gone for more than six hours.

He picked up the phone and called Brett down the road. His friend answered after a few rings.

"Hey Chris, what's going on?"

"Aunt Natalie isn't back yet," Chris said unable to hide the concern in his voice. He'd called Brett right after his aunt peeled out of the driveway.

"My dad isn't too worried," Brett said. "He's known Natalie for a long time. He said not to jump to any conclusions."

"Yeah, but you should have seen her, man," Chris answered. "She was in a rage. I just know she was gonna raise a fuss over there. It's not Old Harris I worry about. It's that assistant of his."

"You mean that guy who's almost as big as Tina? Oh, man, I'm sorry. How's he doin' anyway?"

"Okay, I guess. He's in intensive care. I mean, a whole barn fell on him, you know? But he's one tough dude. Anybody else, and I don't think they'd survived it."

"And you said that *thing* crawled out of the wreckage first?"

"I don't know what that thing was," Chris said slowly, "but yeah, it pushed its way right out of the ruins. That was *tough*, man. I mean, it took the entire fire department to dig Tina out the next morning. That creature just threw those barn beams and boards around like sticks."

Brett exhaled into the phone. "Wow, man. So, what did you tell the cops?"

"We told them what happened," Chris explained. "Then they yelled at us for partying in the woods and destroying private property. And we weren't even the ones who knocked down the barn! Not that anybody lives way out there anyway. I'm not sure anybody actually owns that property. Of course, they didn't believe us about some monster running wild in the woods, no matter how many of us told the story."

"Do you think we should call the police now?" Brett asked.

Thinking carefully for a few moments, Chris finally answered, "No, I don't think so. I'm not sure they'd take me seriously after that last report."

"Are you going to hang out there without her?" Brett asked. "You're welcome to come over if you want, you know."

"Yeah, I'll probably just wait for her here. Your dad's probably right, she'll be home any time now."

"Don't worry, man, she'll be fine," Brett said cheerfully. "Maybe she went shopping or something. She probably just went up to Traverse City. You know the stores up there are open later and all. Maybe she's bringing you a pizza!"

Under normal circumstances, a pizza would be great. Tonight, however, Chris wasn't exactly hungry. He tried to sound cheered up. "Yeah, maybe. I'll talk to you tomorrow, man."

Once he'd hung up the phone, Chris was sure he needed to do something. It wasn't like his aunt to just head out shopping, especially on a Tuesday evening. She always shopped on Thursday morning, since that was when the weekend specials started at Carson's Supermarket in Interlochen. And it was rare that Aunt Natalie ever went to Traverse City. She didn't even make deliveries any more—that was why she had the boys around. But he appreciated Brett trying to justify her absence all the same.

He really didn't think he should call the police. Undoubtedly they would be far too busy up in the big city to worry much about a missing old lady out in Lake Ann. Even if he called anonymously so they wouldn't make the connection to his last police report, Aunt Natalie had been gone for only a few hours, and from watching TV cop shows, Chris seemed to recall that folks weren't really considered missing for at least 24 hours. He didn't know if that was true or not, but it sounded good. *Besides*, he thought, *if it was on TV, it must be pretty accurate, right?* And if something bad had happened to Aunt Natalie, she would need help now, not later on.

"What choice does that leave me?" he asked aloud, and was startled by his own voice echoing through the tall ceiling of the loading area.

But he knew the choice he left himself. Chris was pretty sure his mind had been made up a couple hours ago.

Then he had another thought. He'd call Linda. She should be back at camp by now. He'd already talked to her once since she had given him the direct phone number to the rustic cabin she shared with the little girls. She would give him good advice. If nothing else, it would be nice just to hear her voice.

The line rang twice before an unfamiliar female voice answered.

"Um, hi, is Linda there?"

"No, she hasn't come back yet," the voice informed him. "Can I take a message for her?"

That's really odd, he thought. *She should have been back almost two hours ago.*

"No, that's all right. Did she say when she'd be back by chance?"

"Well," the female voice said, dropping to almost a whisper as she shared the gossip. "She should have been back well before now. I'm covering for her. Our nighttime supervisor is really ticked off. We tried calling over to the Tuscarora Club but there's no answer there. They're not picking up their phones, I guess."

It was Chris's turn to panic now. This wasn't good; not good at all. It was one thing to have Aunt Natalie disappear into that lodge. It was too much of a coincidence that his girlfriend was missing, too. There had to be a connection somehow.

Girlfriend, he mused, momentarily distracted. He'd only known her for a few days, they'd only gone out once (and that was quite a rather wild first date), and yet he was ready to bestow the title upon her.

Hanging up the phone, Chris grabbed his Tigers hat off the counter and the keys to the International from the hook over Natalie's desk. Driving that old beater wouldn't exactly be a sneak attack, but it would be better than walking the three miles in the dark. He could park at the edge of the Tuscarora Club entrance and hike the rest of the way in.

A plan already forming in his mind, Chris also snagged the big flashlight from the hook behind the door. It was always handy, right where he needed it to be. *It's amazing*, he thought. *Aunt Natalie's always so organized, so good at what she does around here. A place for everything, and everything in its place*, he'd heard someplace.

Then the reality of the situation hit him square on.

They need help, I just know it, he thought. *And there's not much time. I don't know how I know, I just do.*

CHAPTER 8
The Last Stand

Overhanging tree branches nearly obscured the light from the crescent moon that had almost reached its zenith in the black sky.

Chris had parked the old International pickup in the tall grass at the edge of the main road. Walking down the winding, quarter-mile driveway leading to the Tuscarora Lodge was like walking through a dark cave.

Aunt Natalie's flashlight provided enough light so that he could see, and it was an easy stroll down the asphalt. However, after the scare they'd had at Tina's bonfire the other night, walking alone in the darkness wasn't just eerie. It was downright terrifying.

Only his mission kept Chris moving forward, his fears of monsters in the woods pushed to the back of his mind. He might be frightened, but he was determined to help his friends.

Now he feared the worst for two of the people he cared about the most here in northern Michigan. Not only had his Aunt Natalie failed to return from the lodge, but his girlfriend had failed to return to her camp. Both should have been back hours earlier. Chris was sure they were both detained here at the lodge; he could just feel it.

I hope Linda didn't do something crazy like trying to take that necklace, he thought.

But if Aunt Natalie was out here, that should get Linda off the hook, even if she did do something rash. *Not necessarily,* Chris thought. Aunt Natalie would never let someone harm a kid, especially a girl. But what if she was incapacitated and couldn't help?

He ran his fingers through his wavy hair and blew out a worried breath. *God, I hope they're both alright.*

After a few more steps with only the flashlight for guidance, his prayer was answered.

However, it was not the answer he was seeking.

An all-too-familiar growl echoed back through the woods from far ahead. It was low and deep, sounding more like an animal giving a warning than a sign of attack. True, this sound wasn't nearly as loud or as nearby as when Chris and his friends had heard it a few nights previously. But there was no mistaking that horrific noise.

Chris stopped in his tracks. He could feel the hairs on his legs and the back of his neck standing straight out. This was the first cool evening all summer, so he had slipped on his jean jacket before leaving his aunt's office. But despite the jacket, goosebumps popped out on his skin, and a shiver ran down his back. Every instinct screamed at him to run, run away, run back to the International and drive anywhere, anywhere but here. For a long second, Chris thought his feet might actually backstep and follow the advice his brain was giving him. Even his shoulders and waist were beginning to pivot, wanting to go back the way he came, and quickly.

But in the end, his sheer will held him rooted to the spot.

Are you sure this is such a good idea? he thought.

I've gotta check on Linda, on Aunt Natalie. If they're in trouble, if they need me and I don't go to them, I'll never be able to live with myself.

Are you sure they're up there? he sighed.

He knew it in his heart that both of them were in the lodge and that they needed help desperately. And with the creature closing in, the entire situation had escalated.

Are you gonna get yourself killed in the process? he asked himself.

He had no answer for that.

Heart racing, Chris realized he was breathing like an asthmatic runner.

His right hand squeezed the shaft of the flashlight and he closed his eyes. Chris exhaled three long, deep breaths slowly into the cool night. And he thought of their faces, picturing every detail of the two women who were potentially in great danger ahead.

Aunt Natalie's wizened, generous face appeared in the darkness of his mind. There were little crowfeet at the corners of her hazel eyes. Her short and thinning gray hair poofed out from under her baseball cap. She was kindhearted, but there was steel there, too. Her grandmotherly spectacles veiled the inner strength and determination of a highly successful businesswoman, one who had to claw and scratch for every inch of achievement.

And Linda was the flame burning in Chris's heart. He still remembered her best from the other evening, sitting at the Dairy Queen picnic table, her chestnut hair absolutely glowing in the setting sun. She smiled easily and often as they talked about movies, music, the summer. He didn't know much about her life away from northern Michigan other than that she preferred to be here rather than there. That did say a lot. He'd meant to ask her more later that evening but it had by then been so rudely interrupted. Having survived the worst first date in history, Chris was not only smitten with her, but he thought it was quite likely he was falling in love.

Another low growl from up ahead brought him from his reverie. His mind had been trying to figure out what it was they'd encountered the other night. Its first appearance in the field on all fours had led Chris to believe it must be a wolf or perhaps a huge, mangy coyote. He'd thought he'd heard somewhere that wolves could stand upright when hunting to get a better look at or size up its prey. And hey, didn't people train their dogs to stand up on hind legs or prance around their living rooms to get treats and impress guests? But Chris also had heard that this standing posture could only be held for a few seconds at most. Even a well-trained pet could only take a few steps before falling back down. And there was no wolf, no dog, no other canine that could walk or run on its two hind legs like a man.

A connection to a wolf wasn't quite right anyway. It wasn't exactly a werewolf or a wolfman, at least not like those in the old monster movies he'd watched as a kid. He'd seen so many of those films on the Saturday late show. Those were just cheesy Hollywood special effects. This thing was so much more. And it was real! It wasn't just the movie magic that brought this creature to life.

And it was no normal animal, far more supernatural than simply a gigantic wolf or a wild dog.

Dog...Dogman. Yeah, that seemed to make the best sense. He didn't know if giving it a name made it less of a horror or not. He'd heard someplace that naming your fear lead to conquering that fear. Chris wasn't sure that would be true in this case.

Still, the young man hurried along the winding driveway. It took all of his courage to keep going, knowing that the horrific creature was somewhere in the darkness ahead of him.

But likely his girlfriend and aunt were up there, too. And if they were in the lodge as he feared, they were undoubtedly in several kinds of danger.

***

The four black gemstones sat on the edge of a long sofa table a little bit away. They almost seemed to be taunting Natalie. *So close and yet so far away.*

The old man had pulled out his Smith & Wesson .38-caliber snub-nose revolver from the wheelchair's inner pocket. The weapon was trained on Natalie while Braydon finished the last knot. The old woman was fully secured to the wooden chair.

"You won't get away with this," she growled at the two men. "What are you going to do, kill us?" She looked momentarily over to the girl still passed out in the chair next to her.

"There are other ways to make someone disappear, Natalie," the old man replied. He looked up at Braydon, and for the first time, the big man's chiseled face gave a hint of a smile. "Trust me," Harris went on, "this isn't the first time someone's meddled in my plans. We have contingencies for everything."

Harris might have been ready to expose more of his plans, but he was interrupted by a deep, menacing growl emanating from just outside the lodge's front entrance.

"What is that?" the old man asked loudly. In their sound-proofed rooms upstairs, neither Harris nor Braydon had heard the nightly screams and howls that had been echoing across the countryside for the past few weeks.

Aunt Natalie looked toward the front of the lodge, her eyes opened widely. She'd heard that noise before and even thought she knew what it might be. She gulped in a way that might have seemed comical under different circumstances. That growl was far too close for comfort. Looking at the claw-shaped gemstones, she thought she saw them glow a faint reddish color for just a brief moment.

And then, the entire world erupted in chaos.

The front entrance literally exploded. Both of the heavy oak entry doors blew inward, tearing free from their hinges. One slammed against the adjacent wall where it cracked neatly in two. The other door soared across the foyer and all the way into the great hall, where it smashed a game table and two chairs. Chess pieces mingled with oak splinters of all sizes.

All eyes locked on the creature that emerged out of the dust. It was at least seven and a half feet tall, even with its legs slightly bent at the knees. Its canine-shaped head hung low, its muzzle open, teeth bared and panting. It stared back at them, and then took a couple of measured, powerful steps in the room.

"What contingency plan do you have for this?" Natalie inquired loudly to the old man, her eyebrows raised. She chuckled, mocking him. "You gonna make him disappear, too?"

But Harris was silent, his eyes open in fear.

On the other hand, if Braydon was afraid, he didn't show it. Though the monster was a little taller than Harris's big assistant, Braydon was thicker in the chest, shoulders, and arms. He peeled off his light flannel shirt and dropped it on the stone floor. Then he cracked his knuckles, muscles bulging in his arms, and strode forward confidently to challenge the beast.

***

The loud destruction of the lodge's front entry could be heard all around the property. On Lake Doubennet, a pair of squawking ducks flew up out of the water. A lone raccoon sprinted off through the woods, chattering anxiously the whole way, until it actually ran into the fence that separated the Tuscarora Club property from the acreage owned by Camp Doubennet. It fell backward, stunned by the impact.

Chris was nearly to the Tuscarora Club's parking lot when the creature stepped inside and bellowed. The young man sucked in a deep breath of the northern Michigan air. From the motion lights on the front porch, Chris could see the devastation the creature had caused. The front doors were completely gone, torn right from their hinges. A light cloud of dust was still settling in the entry light.

The Dogman was here.

Though he was very worried about Linda and Aunt Natalie, Chris wasn't about to go charging right in behind the monster. Instead, he sprinted around the left side of the huge building, nimbly leaping right over the recently trimmed bushes.

Since the ground sloped down to the lake, the staircase up to the long back deck was four times as high as the front pair of steps. Chris took them two at a time, anxious to see inside the lodge through the big glass doors. It was the only other way he knew how to get into the building.

***

It was a battle of the ages. With the exception of being recently blindsided a few nights before, the Dogman had not encountered such a powerful or crafty foe as this human in a long, long time. No matter how hard the creature tried to get its deadly claws into Braydon's skin, the human parried or slipped away. The human was obviously a well-trained warrior, despite his resemblance to the other soft-looking humans of this age.

The Dogman and the human tumbled their way across the room, smashing furniture and shredding the pillows and fabrics. One pillow was clawed open and feathers poofed around in all directions. Braydon used everything his hands could grasp as a weapon, knowing he didn't want to get too close to those lethal claws. He swung shattered table slats and even broke chairs over the Dogman's body. But the beast could take a beating while continuing its advance.

At one point, the skirmish moved past the kitchen, with Braydon backpedaling and the Dogman in pursuit. Harris's big assistant, finding no other weapon easily at hand, grasped a tall kerosene lamp sitting on an end table. He hurled it at the beast. But the Dogman's reflexes were much too quick. In a graceful move, one clawed hand simply redirected the lamp and sent it sailing into the pass-through fireplace. The lamp's porcelain base, once a decoratively painted antique from Switzerland, smashed against the inside of the stone fireplace, its volatile contents spraying liquid fire into the kitchen.

In just a few seconds, the kerosene from that little lantern started a blaze that spread throughout the entire kitchen.

The old man had his .38 out, trying to get into position for a decent shot at the creature. Harris made it a habit to keep himself protected at all times, and though he had never had to pull the gun in a real situation, he had practiced his sharp shooting many times. He was finding out that moving targets were far more difficult shots than he'd ever imagined. He wheeled one direction only to have the pair of battlers move away or to find Braydon end up directly in the line of sight.

Then as Harris watched, the two combatants tumbled up against the sofa and table where the precious gemstones were lying.

The Dogman had just caught sight of the razor-claws, the *itZic shileeteh* that it had been seeking, and its eyes widened eagerly. Ignoring the human, the beast reached forward, trying to grasp the treasures.

Capitalizing on the distraction, Braydon thumped one powerful fist into the Dogman's lower jaw. It was a well-placed blow, and probably would have knocked out a mere human. The creature's head whipped upward from the impact. Braydon continued the onslaught, slamming his shoulder into the beast's chest. The two teetered on the edge of the sofa right above the table with the gemstones lying peacefully below.

Harris tried to wheel himself to the table but he was far too late. The two huge bodies fell onto its far edge, and the table became a catapult. Both Natalie and Harris yelled "No!" as the four gemstones flew high into the air, scattering themselves among the mess of wood and dust that was now settling all over the lodge's floor.

***

Peering through the glass doors on the lodge's lake side, Chris was shocked at what he saw within. Of course, his attention was drawn to the melee currently destroying most of the great hall, and to the ball of fire that had erupted from the fireplace. Braydon and the Dogman were fighting, each trading blows. But Chris could see the big man was slowing down.

Then two gunshots echoed through the room and Chris instinctively jerked back from the glass. The old man had shot the creature, and its body rocked back from the impact. But after a few moments, the Dogman resumed its attack on Braydon.

And then, as he scanned the room, Chris found what he'd come for. He could see his aunt tied to a wooden chair, her back to him. Her shoulders, legs, and wrists were wriggling as she tried her best to free herself, apparently with no luck. And slumped in a dark brown recliner, Chris could see the very top of someone's head, wisps of familiar light brown hair lying limply against the recliner. It had to be Linda. He had no idea of her condition, since she wasn't moving at all.

With everything going on in there, maybe I can slip in without drawing attention to myself, he thought.

***

Braydon was very quick for a man of his size. He did manage to dodge the Dogman's slashing claws and teeth, though he couldn't totally avoid the blows from the creature's arms.

The Dogman caught Braydon square across the jaw and spun him around. His balance lost, the big man slipped to his knees. There, on the floor, Braydon saw one of the sharp, black gemstones from that necklace the girl had stolen. These claw-shaped stones were as long and sharp as a knife, and they'd be better than his fists. He snagged it with his left hand thinking, *Maybe this'll be useful. Nothing else has worked so far.*

Trying to regain his footing, he reached his right arm up to push off one of the heavy, rectangular tables that had yet sustained damage. At that moment, the Dogman slammed its fist down, embedding Braydon's arm into the table top. A sickening crunch issued forth as the arm bones snapped and immediately afterward, the top of the table cracked.

The big man screamed loudly, but despite the intense pain, he slashed his left hand upward. The claw-shaped stone sliced deeply into the creature's forearm. It jumped back, howling in its own pain and releasing the human, who then staggered to his feet. Dark maroon blood sprayed in all directions, soaking Braydon's white t-shirt.

At the same moment, a gun shot blasted through the hall, and the Dogman's shoulder rocked backward. Another shot, and a spray of blood appeared, this time the drops splattering one of the glass display cases. The bullet missed the glass, however, and tore a chunk out of one of the huge cedar logs in the wall. The Dogman looked up in surprise to see the old, balding man in the wheeled chair pointing his weapon, smoke still issuing from its barrel.

Harris would have gotten off another shot but Braydon was in the way. The big man had regained a bit of his swagger. Even with a broken and battered right arm that was basically useless, he'd found a weapon that seemed very effective against the creature. He intended to see how much damage he could do with it.

***

Chris carefully turned the door knob and quietly opened the french door. As expected, he went in unnoticed. Old Harris continued to wheel about looking to get off another shot, while his assistant was getting in some good blows with some sort of small knife. The Dogman was bleeding, profusely in some places. But Braydon was fighting with only one arm, and was slowly losing ground despite his best maneuvers.

Immediately, Chris could smell the fire, though there was no real visible smoke yet. But something in the lodge was burning big time. Adrenaline started pumping through his system. He half crouched, half crawled around the furniture until he was right behind the two women. He could see Aunt Natalie was her same old ornery self, desperately struggling with the ropes. Her face contorted with the effort. Chris knew that being tied up only made her more irritable.

Linda appeared much worse off. She was out cold in the recliner. There was an accusing red line around her neck where Chris was sure the necklace had been torn off of her. *So she did get a hold of Aunt Natalie's necklace,* he thought. *Girl's got spunk, that's for sure.* Since his aunt was awake, he'd start with her.

Poking his head up from behind the chair in which his aunt was tied, he whispered, "Are you okay?"

Aunt Natalie swung her head around, recognizing his voice. "I'll be better when you get us out of here," she whispered back.

"How about Linda?" Chris couldn't hide the concern in his voice.

"Yeah. She's still unconscious. Take her first." Aunt Natalie nodded over toward Linda. "Get her out of here. This place is getting way too out of hand. Then come get me. I'll be fine till you get back."

"You sure?"

"Get going!" she commanded. Though her voice was still very soft, there was steel behind it. "That big guy won't last long." She looked off toward the kitchen, where a red-orange glow could be seen through both the pass-through fireplace and the round windows of the twin swinging, restaurant-style doors. "Besides, I think we may have other problems soon."

With the chaos ensuing in the main hall, Chris was able to scoop up Linda's inert body, drag her over the back of the recliner, and sneak to the double doors leading out to the deck over the lake. With the toe of one tennis shoe, he opened the door just wide enough to slip through. Though Linda's frame was rather small, Chris was still straining to carry her out away from the lodge. He lay her body down on the deck a dozen feet away from the water, wishing he could move her much farther away. But he had to get back inside to his Aunt Natalie. At least she was conscious and he wouldn't have to carry her.

***

Harris Wellington lined up the creature in his sights for the perfect shot. Its back was turned to him. It was the right time. Harris envisioned the shot, right to the base of the creature's neck, just above the shoulder blades. The old man squinted one eye and looked right down his arm and past the .38's short barrel. He held the weapon securely with two hands. The creature was less than 20 feet away, its attention fully turned to Braydon. Harris gritted his teeth and grinned at the creature as he pulled the trigger.

Click. Click-click.

The gun didn't fire. The chamber was empty!

Frustrated, Harris swore loudly and then began searching the pockets of his wheelchair for more bullets.

***

Less than a minute later, Chris had his aunt free. The two were ducking low behind the remaining unbroken furniture. Above them, a thin veil of smoke was beginning to blanket the hall.

"Let's go," Chris whispered.

But his aunt shook her head. "Not without my necklace. You go ahead."

Chris couldn't believe her. "I'm not leaving you here," he whispered forcibly.

"Then help me find those gemstones," she insisted, crawling on her hands and knees and beginning to sift through the debris.

***

Across the room, Braydon, groaning in pain, was forced to his knees. The huge man's battered right arm hung loosely at his side, his left wrist was still gripped tightly in the Dogman's clawed hand. Rivulets of blood streamed down Braydon's arm as the claws dug deeply into his flesh. Finally, he could hold out no longer. Braydon's fist popped open, fingers exhausted, exposing the treasure within.

The Dogman snarled in delight, its eyes widening at the sight of the *itZic shileeteh,* the ancient and sacred razor-claw, lying still in the human's open palm. Deftly, the creature plucked it up with its other hand. Dropping its grip on the human, the Dogman raised the black gemstone up to its eyes, inspecting it carefully.

Below, Braydon made one last act of defiance. From the miscellany covering the lodge floor, he grasped a broken, wooden shaft that had once been a chair leg. With his last bit of strength, he stabbed the sharpened spear of wood into the back of the Dogman's leg, just above the knee joint. His hand was instantly covered with the creature's thick, maroon blood.

An ear-splitting howl of pain echoed loudly through the lodge. Both Natalie and Chris had to cover their ears with their hands as the awful sound pierced them right to the bone.

A second later, the Dogman crouched, its free hand pulling the shaft of wood free from its leg. It looked down at the man and curled up its lip, exposing its dripping fangs.

Braydon gave one last exhausted breath. His head dropped back and his eyes closed, oblivious to what happened next.

The Dogman's hand dropped the bloody chair leg and then swung upward, claws opened and whistling through the air. Four deep gashes opened on Braydon's chest and neck as blood spurted in all directions. The big man's body actually rose up off the ground from the impact, and then fell limply to the stone floor a few feet away.

***

Reloading the little pistol seemed to take forever. The old man's shaking fingers kept dropping the bullets down into his wheelchair seat.

He was now sitting in the very center of the great hall, able to see the devastation in all directions around him. The place was in shambles. When he turned his head to the left, Harris Wellington noticed that the two prisoners were gone. But a few feet away, there was a newcomer to the party. Harris had no idea when this young man had arrived or where he had come from. The women were gone, this young man was here, and he was holding two of the black gemstones that had taken the old man so long to acquire.

Harris's sanity was teetering and he was oblivious to everything else. The world was collapsing around him. It didn't matter that his great lodge, his life's greatest achievement, was on fire. It didn't matter that the two prisoners, witnesses to all sorts of crimes he'd been committing, had escaped. It didn't matter that his assistant was currently being ripped to shreds by a nightmarish creature.

All of his concentration was on this young kid who was holding the black treasures. These accursed gemstones were the cause of all of this chaos. And now, they were in this kid's hands.

The old man finally snapped. In a rage, he raised the gun and pointed it at the young man. Harris didn't know who this kid was, but he was going to pay for everything that had gone wrong this evening.

***

Chris turned to show his aunt that he acquired the other two gemstones. She'd flashed him the first gemstone she'd found earlier, giving him the thumbs up with a grin. They had been crawling over the floor, under the tables, frantically looking for the treasures while keeping down out of the ever-building layer of smoke. The fourth gemstone had already been taken from Braydon by the Dogman. But instead of being able to flash Aunt Natalie a thumbs up, Chris found himself staring right back down the barrel of the old man's gun. He froze, knowing there was no way he could outrun a bullet, knowing that he was far too close for the old man to miss.

And suddenly, Aunt Natalie came to the rescue. She appeared at Harris's side brandishing a kitchen broom she'd found who knows where. The old man had just enough time to look up at her, startled, before she struck.

It was a perfect swing. She was gripping the broom just above the thistles and the meat of the handle made contact with the old man's face right between his upper teeth and continued up into his nostrils. Harris's dentures were smashed instantly, and the cartilage in his nose caved in. For a brief moment, as the broom handle shattered and then wrapped around his head, his face went as flat as the wall. Then the impact was gone, and the skin of his nose sagged back down.

The old man's eyes rolled back up behind his eyelids, and his head fell to his chest, unconscious.

How does she do that? Chris asked himself, relieved that she'd appeared out of nowhere to save his life. And then a movement caught Chris's eyes. "Duck!" he yelled at the top of his lungs.

Chris had never seen his Aunt Natalie move so quickly. He didn't think she still had it in her. But she'd already surprised him several times this evening. Her reaction speed was very impressive.

Natalie ducked to her knees and swung the broken broom handle upward to protect herself.

It was just at the right moment, because the Dogman had not anticipated her move. It soared through the space she'd just occupied and recalculated its leap upon landing. The beast turned with a single hop and sprung straight back up, very high into the air, intending to attack from above.

But the air space right above the creature was occupied by the lodge's great chandelier. This also caught the Dogman by surprise, and unable to change direction, the beast landed upon the massive, intricate structure. Its clawed feet smashed right through the two lowest levels. The Dogman's clawed hands grabbed for purchase on the upper levels, finally latching hold of a wooden beam. Antlers, broken light bulbs, and bits of wooden superstructure rained down, bouncing off the stone floor nearly 15 feet below. Chris ran forward, grasped Natalie's wrist, and pulled her away.

Even though the chandelier was tightly bolted to the ceiling, the added weight of the Dogman was too much for it. Two of the three support wires snapped immediately, and as the chandelier tilted, the beast had already pulled its feet back up, able to push against one of the only solid support wheels still structurally sound.

The creature shoved itself off the chandelier and leaped in a somersault to the far side of the hall just in time. The third and final wire tore free sending the heavy structure quickly to the floor, crushing and burying old Harris and his wheelchair beneath its tumbled mass.

Chris and Natalie turned their backs on the rush of dust, glass shards, sharp bone fragments, and splinters that flew in all directions.

Still coughing from the dust, Chris reached out and placed his two gemstones into his aunt's hand.

"Good work," she said between spastic coughs.

We're not done yet, Chris thought as they heard the beast's growl from the other side of the smashed chandelier near the lodge's lakeside doors.

***

For the briefest second, while getting his bearings, Chris thought he saw a face, an all-too-familiar-looking face, peering in from a window on the lakeside wall behind the creature. It was a plain, easily forgettable face, mostly covered by black aviator-style sunglasses, and yet it was a face Chris was sure that he'd seen somewhere before. But after the young man blinked from the slowly building smoke in the room, he saw nothing there anymore. There was no time to wonder about that now, they needed to get out fast.

Natalie stood her ground, her feet firmly planted. If she was scared, she certainly didn't show it. She still clutched the handle of the broom, as if that insignificant, broken tool could be of any detriment to the monster again. *Probably wouldn't do much damage to a person let alone this thing*, Chris thought. Natalie's right hand was still balled into a fist.

The old woman took a quick breath through clenched teeth. When she spoke, the words came out harsh and authoritative. "Stop right there!"

Chris gulped as the Dogman turned its attention to them. Never in his life had he been more terrified. Here they were, in great danger of being burned to death, and the old lady was calling to it! She'd managed to block their only escape route.

The creature was still crouched over, knuckles dangling near its hairy knees.

"I know whatchoo want," Natalie continued, unabashed. "I know whatcher after. I got it right here."

And with that, she opened her fist. Lying upon her palm, contrasting with her white, wrinkly skin, were the three black jewels.

The creature's face lit up with surprise (and Chris thought, perhaps an all-too-human show of pleasure). Its golden eyes opened wide, amplified by the reflection of the bright fire all around. Drool seeped down between its jaws. The Dogman stared at the old woman, or more specifically, at the prize she held out. Slowly, it advanced, one canine foot after another. Despite the roar of the blaze, the claws clicked loudly on the stone floor.

Chris was speechless, caught in the creature's spell. He saw its arms widen, palms forward, claws opening and closing slowly. Even as it strode forward, walking around the smashed chandelier and kicking aside broken pieces of furniture, its knees were slightly bending, building up power in its legs. It would spring at any moment, unleashing its fury. And there was no place for them to go, no place to escape. Chris could only watch, terrified and helpless, unable to croak out even a warning.

But Natalie was not fooled. The old woman clenched her fist again, hiding the sharpened jewels. She pushed the broom out at the Dogman, like some sort of weird talisman, warding him back. "Stop right there!" she commanded, and as a surprise to all, the creature did just that. Only 15 feet away, it straightened up to its full height and stared down at the woman.

Chris's jaw dropped open and he could only stare at the scene. *How does she do that?* he wondered again, now for the umpteenth time.

However, the young man knew that there was still very little to celebrate. The curtains around the front entry had been alighted, and now the interior walls were catching fire. Smoke was already pouring relentlessly into the great hall from the kitchen area, and the ceiling was nearly obscured.

In a very athletic move that Chris wouldn't have believed possible for a woman her age, Natalie flung the cursed jewels at the Dogman. Of course, his aunt had been amazing him all night. Her arm and wrist snapped like a pitcher firing a fastball. *Doesn't throw like a girl,* Chris thought to himself, smiling inside.

At that same moment, an explosion rocked the lodge from the kitchen. The restaurant-styled double doors took the brunt of the blast, snapping wide open as the superheated air forced its way through.

The jewels, sailing through the air at the time of the blast, were lost for a moment in time. Two of the sharpened claw-like gems twirled end over end, sparkling in the light from the fire behind. The twinkle contrasted with the dull black exterior.

Nimbly, the Dogman plucked these two out of the air with its right claw.

The third jewel sailed away from its companions. Chris watched, fascinated, as its deep dark shape was backlit by the golden orange flame issuing from the kitchen doors. The jewel neither tumbled nor spun, but remained straight, its sharply pointed end upright and cutting the air as it quickly traversed the room.

But the Dogman was quicker once again. Though its body stayed put, its right arm extended, reaching wide and revealing a tremendous wingspan. Deadly sharp claws opened wide, just far enough to snag the final jewel in its furry fingers. The Dogman turned its head downward as the two clawed hands brought the treasures together in front of its muscled chest. Chris wasn't sure, but he thought the creature had the hints of a smile at the corners of its muzzle.

"Now, you git!" Natalie shouted. "Git out! Leave this place! Leave us alone!" she shrieked at the creature.

The Dogman snapped its head up, evil glowing eyes glaring at the old woman. They locked glares, a battle of the ages raging between their upturned faces.

There was power in the old woman's voice, an old and ancient authority. One hand still held the broom handle, but the other was flashing the creature some ancient hand signal with two fingers up and spread while two others were curled in. Her commanding attitude, her fearless posture, and her defiant stance was the kind of presence that the creature had not encountered in a millennium or more.

A deep growling built up in the Dogman's throat. It narrowed its eyes and curled its lips, revealing the long, curving canine teeth. A snorting snarl shot out like a warning across the distance.

It all happened so fast. One moment Chris was watching the scene unfold like a showdown in an old Western movie. The next moment the creature was already in the air.

The Dogman had sprung forward in a high arc, the massive wingspan of its arms spread wide to catch its prey. Its deadly fangs were bared.

The two humans tumbled into each other as they instinctively ducked. Both turned their heads down, fully expecting the crushing blow, the piercing fangs, the ripping claws. Natalie's left hand held the broom overhead as if that would protect them.

Chris squinted his eyes and ground his teeth awaiting the end.

But instead, the creature completely sailed over the two humans and landed with a thud on the stone floor behind them. Chris heard the clicking of its toe claws on the stone. As he rolled over, he managed one quick glance and saw the monster. Its paws were still closed in fists, tightly clutching its treasure. It couldn't have attacked without losing the jewels! Besides, it had what it wanted, and the humans were of no consequence. Ignoring them now, and not looking back, it soared through the flames encircling the main entrance with one long low leap. Then it was gone.

***

The heat was becoming nearly unbearable, and Chris and Natalie couldn't help but cough from the smoke that had completely filled the upper levels and was now settling down to the main floor. Chris grabbed the old woman's arm, surprised at the strength of the muscles beneath her flannel shirt.

"We gotta go!" he yelled over the roaring of the fire. "Come on!"

Natalie snapped out of the spell and for the first time seemed to realize what was going on around them. But she hardly seemed worried. In fact, she was amazingly calm. Later on, Chris would wonder if she'd been in shock or if she really was totally in charge of the situation the entire time.

Every exit was blocked by fire and smoke. The only way out of the lodge was through the doors to the lake. Besides, Linda was still out there. Linda! In all of the action here, he'd almost forgotten her. Knowing he had to make sure she was okay, Chris tugged, and the old woman picked up the pace.

Somewhere close by there was a loud crash as one balcony collapsed. Sparks and debris flew in all directions, a few singing holes in Natalie's shirt.

The fire had escaped the walls of the lodge, and both the outside shrubbery and the deck's side staircase that Chris had scaled earlier were aflame. There was no escape to either side.

Linda was still lying unconscious on the deck, oblivious to everything going on around her.

"The lake!" cried the young man as a fresh explosion blew out the glass of the upper floors.

Natalie paused at the edge of the deck, looking down at the black water of the lake. A sparkle of the crescent moon's reflection rippled on its surface.

There was no time for debate. Chris pushed the old woman off the deck. There was a surprised gasp just before she plunged into the cold water.

He took one last look at the great lodge. For a moment, he thought he felt the entire building take a breath of air inward. "Not good," he panted, knowing what was coming. There was no time left.

In one quick move, just like fielding a ground ball, he scooped up Linda's limp body and leapt into the air. It was not a moment too soon.

As the roof collapsed, the lodge bellowed out its greatest explosion, lighting up the night. Shards of glass blew in all directions from the few remaining windows. The doors were reduced to splinters shooting out through the night, some embedding themselves in the bark of nearby trees.

***

Only one person watched the whole scene play out. The mysterious man behind the black aviator sunglasses saw it all clearly from his vantage point behind the boat house. Carefully, he slipped his infrared binoculars into their side holster. Then he pulled his little recorder to his lips and spoke briefly into its microphone. A few seconds later, he slipped back into the darkness, his business at the lodge done.

Though he'd hiked in through the woods, he took the winding entry driveway back to his government-issue sedan, which was parked, well hidden, down the main road. However, halfway back to his vehicle, he found something was blocking his path.

It was a rather large, hairy something, and its growling was interspersed with rasped breaths.

The mystery man was only a bit surprised. He'd almost been expecting this. But watching and observing the creature from a distance was nothing like encountering it in person. On the outside, the man was still all business. However, his calm demeanor hid the fear that soared through his body. Sure, he'd been studying this creature for years, but until right now, he'd never been this close to it.

The Dogman stepped forward, still growling. It reached out its right paw and grabbed the man by the lapels of his black suit jacket. The claws tightened, drawing the fabric so close together that the man could hardly breathe. The man's hands gripped the hairy wrist of the beast, finding it unyielding. Then the Dogman flexed its arm muscles and lifted the man a foot off the ground, bringing him up to eye level.

Feet dangling, the man struggled to pull out a chain from under the white collar of his dress shirt. Not a moment too soon, he'd removed his own necklace and flashed a charm of his own before the eyes of the creature.

Immediately, the Dogman dropped the man, repelled by the talisman he wore around his neck. Though he fell back onto his butt, the man quickly stood back up. "You know what this is, don't you?" he asked the creature, holding the amulet out to the length of the chain necklace. "You've seen it before."

Squinting, its eyes reduced to glowing slits, the Dogman wrinkled up its muzzle, exposing its fangs. It gave the human one last gritty snarl, and then it bounded away into the darkness.

"We'll meet again, I'm sure," the mysterious man spoke into the darkness.

***

The only scream the old woman made that entire night was heard as she burst up to the surface for air. The cold water had nearly knocked the wind from her chest.

Chris came to the surface still cradling the now struggling Linda in his arms. She was wide awake now and completely unsure of where she was or how she got there.

From the water, the great lodge looked like something from a horror movie. It was an enormous, deformed alien skull with flames pouring forth from its many eye sockets. It seemed to be breathing fire, as debris shot out from the three door openings on the ground floor, the pillars between each resembling teeth. Above, the collapsed roof left a cavity that blazed 20 feet up into the night air, looking like a lunatic's spastic wiry hair blowing in the breeze.

And somewhere in the forest behind the inferno, only adding to the horrific scene, the Dogman howled once again in triumph, deep and long into the north woods darkness.

Lake Doubennet stayed shallow for quite a distance, and the three people stood in water up to their armpits.

"You okay?" Chris called over to his aunt, who was still catching her breath. "That was impressive, you standin' up to that creature like that." He could still hardly believe she'd triumphed over the Dogman.

"I ain't afraid of no man or no dog," she smiled. "Never have been."

The young man turned to Linda whose arms were encircling his neck. Even in the darkness, he could see her eyes twinkle and a smile spread across her face. "So, do you think we can finally have that kiss?" he asked.

In the background, the great lodge continued to burn, all traces of the Wellington empire becoming merely ash and sparks blowing up into the north woods night. In a few seconds, they heard the welcoming sound of wailing sirens begin to echo through the trees.

"I think this is the perfect time and place," Linda answered him, closing her eyes and raising her lips to his.

EPILOGUE

What it is, bro," Tina said weakly, adding in a cough. He barely fit in the hospital bed. As it was, his feet stuck out several inches over the end at the bottom.

Chris slapped the big man five. "How soon before you get outta this place, man?"

"I gotta say, the food ain't that great, but the scenery is pretty nice." With that, Tina's eyes and face turned to follow the very cute, young nurse who was just leaving the room. She gave him a sly look back over her shoulder to accompany an equally sly smile.

"Yeah, she can't get enough of me," Tina went on. "But they're probably gonna kick me out in a day or so. Punctured lung is nothin' to laugh at, you know. "

"Hey, I brought you something." Chris handed a package to the big man. "I had it made just for you."

"You're gonna love it," Linda said, patting Tina's arm.

"Am I?" Tina said his eyebrows raised in wonderment.

Tina wasted no time tearing off the wrapping paper.

"Check it out," Chris nodded, smiling at his big friend. He had his arm around his girlfriend's waist.

Tina's huge arms held the t-shirt up so he could admire it. His bearded face lit up in a huge smile. "That's really cool, man!" He spun it around so both Chris and Linda could see it in all of its glory.

It was a regular white short-sleeve t-shirt. Directly in the center of the front of the shirt was a horrific and slightly demonic-looking wolf's head, layered in tones of black, dark gray, maroon, and purple. Its muzzle was wide open and displaying its sharp fangs. The artist who drew it even added in the slightly turned-up lips to create the faintest of smiles. The wolf's eyes were a fluorescent yellow, finishing it all off. Above the logo were the words MAD WOLVES, and below the logo it said, OF GRAND TRAVERSE COUNTY. The back of the shirt was lettered with BOAR'S HEAD BAR above a large number 1.

"We thought you could use this as the uniform for your next softball team," said Linda, beaming. "Chris says you're quite the slugger."

"Yeah, I'm in it for the long ball, you know. This is really great, you guys," Tina said, still delighted. Then he dropped his arms and laid the t-shirt on his lap. "How's your aunt, bro?" he asked cautiously.

Chris was a little surprised, since no one had really inquired about Aunt Natalie. "She's fine, I guess. The paramedics treated her for a bit of smoke inhalation, the same as me. But she was back at work the next day."

"That's good, man," Tina answered, now sounding a little tired. "She's a good lady."

"She's the best," Chris and Linda both said at the same time, and they broke out in laughter. By the time they were done laughing, Tina was already asleep, his t-shirt tucked in the crook of his right arm like a child's blanket.

Linda slipped her hand into Chris's and smiled up into his bright eyes and nodded toward the door. The young couple quietly slipped out of the hospital room and slowly meandered down the brightly lit hallway.

Chris's thoughts wandered. *Where had the creature come from? Where did it go? Would it ever be seen again?*

He didn't have any idea about his first two questions, but he felt the answer to that last question was a definite yes. He felt it deep in his gut. The Dogman would be back.

The creature was so very interested in the black gemstones from his aunt's old necklace. Aunt Natalie refused to talk about it. But Chris was able to put a few pieces of the puzzle together. The necklace was a treasure, likely something sacred, handed down from Aunt Natalie's Omeena ancestors. Once the Dogman gained possession of the gemstones, it immediately left. Those were what it was after all along.

So, were there more of these gemstones for the creature to find? Who knows? Were there more pieces to this puzzle that had yet to surface? Quite likely. Would he ever encounter the Dogman again? He certainly hoped not. And who belonged to that mysterious face behind the dark sunglasses? Chris was sure he'd really seen that strange man, not just in the lodge window during the fire but at least once before. *What did he want? He'd shown up at the same time as the creature and disappeared just as suddenly. He had to have some connection to this whole mystery.*

"Whatcha thinkin' about?" Linda asked, looking up at her boyfriend.

Chris popped back into the real world. He smiled at Linda and said, "Oh, just thinkin' 'bout how lucky I am to have such great friends, to have a great family like Aunt Natalie, and to have you here with me."

"And now you have to head home for your senior year," she smiled slyly at him.

He winked at her. "Yeah, not everyone gets to go run off to an Ivy League school and be a crazy freshman, you know. Some of us still have to suffer for another year."

"What about Camp Doubennet?"

Chris beamed. "When Champ got a little hint that his property was sitting right atop one of the biggest oil-producing areas in northern Michigan," he said, nodded to Linda, "he had a crew from BP in camp the very next day doing all sorts of tests. Well, turns out selling some of his mineral rights will more than take care of Camp Doubennet for decades. And it just so happens that the paperwork for the deed transfer mysteriously disappeared in the Tuscarora Lodge fire. It was never recorded in the county courthouse, so it's just as if the deal had never happened."

Linda smiled up at him. "Amazing how everything worked out in the end, isn't it?"

Chris nodded, his thoughts briefly stealing him away again. For the rest of his life, he'd wonder just exactly what that creature was that had haunted the summer of 1977. It wasn't an animal, and it wasn't a man, and yet, it wasn't exactly some weird mix of the two either. It was its own being, something real and deadly, yet supernatural and nightmarish. *It's not that it doesn't belong here in northern Michigan*, he thought, *it really doesn't belong here on earth.*

But he had many years into the future to ponder the events of the past few weeks. For now, life was good. He gave Linda's hand a good squeeze and kissed the tip of her nose as the two of them walked out of the hospital and into the warm sunshine of a late August in northern Michigan.

AUTHOR'S NOTE

I first came across the folklore of Michigan's Dogman several years ago. My family was visiting my parents' cabin, deep in the woods. The first snow of the year was falling in early October, which really isn't that much of a freak occurrence, especially if you've lived in northern Michigan for any length of time. The snowflakes were large enough to activate the motion sensor lights outside. It was a surreal scene, the strobe effect of white snowflakes against the deep, dark background of the trees and woods. Anyway, Steve Cook's "The Legend" played on the radio, and normally I do not listen to country music. But that's the station my dad had on. The song absolutely struck a chord with me. I was amazed, I was frightened, I was struck by the power of the imagination.

However, when I actually went out looking for more lore on the Dogman, I found there was nothing. The first novel, <u>Year of the Dogman</u>, actually began as a series of short stories I put together for my students at school. It was really their idea to link them together 'just so' and form a full length novel.

I never in my wildest dreams thought it would take off the way it did. My friend Steve Cook often says the same thing. Sometimes he can't believe his April Fool's joke has lasted over 20 years. And yet, maybe it's not so surprising.

Everywhere I go to share the legend, aspiring authors undoubtedly stop me and ask where I got my inspiration, how long did it all take, how did I find the perseverance to do it?

In think that, maybe, it just takes a leap of faith sometimes.

Some folks talk about luck. I think you tend to make your own luck. When you can put yourself in the right place at the right time, and you have the guts to take that leap, that's what luck is really, isn't it?

So, is there really a Dogman out there running amok in Michigan (or in other places in the world)? A few years ago, I've have said no way. Now, however, I do have to wonder. I've had the unique opportunity to interview dozens of witnesses, people who have seen many strange and sometimes horrific things. The stories are all generally similar. The witnesses seem, for the most part, sincere and honest. They aren't looking for money or notoriety. Some are even shy about their stories, afraid that even I won't believe them. Most people may not know exactly what it was they saw, but they always know it wasn't a person, a deer, or a bear. After that, they weren't sure. But many were badly frightened by their experiences.

I like to think that maybe, as the ruling species on our planet, we haven't discovered everything yet.

Remember, until recent times, such creatures as the mountain gorilla, the panda, the giant squid, these were all folklore creatures. Who's to say other cryptids won't find a home in science after all?

But until then, I think it is important for people to keep that sense of wonderment, that imagination, that fear of the dark. There are so many millions of acres of wilderness all over the world, places where there are no roads, no houses, no people. It's easy to believe that something could be lurking out there, maybe even just out of sight, just at the fringes of the wild, only a step or two away from civilization. I think people want to believe, that we as humans have a *need* to believe. We have a need to tell stories about what mysteries may still exist in the world.

ABOUT THE AUTHOR

With an English degree from Michigan State University and a master's in educational leadership from Central Michigan University, Frank Holes, Jr. teacher literature, writing, and mythology at the middle school level and was recently named a regional teacher of the year. He lives in northern Michigan with his wife Michele, son James, and daughter Sarah.

Frank's first two books in the Dogman series have seen tremendous success in and around the Great Lakes region. And his children's fantasy series, The Longquist Adventures, has been a hit with elementary students through adults.

See all of Frank's novels on his website:

http://www.mythmichigan.com

ABOUT THE COVER ARTIST

Craig Tollenaar lives in southwest Michigan with his wife Traci and his daughters Isobel and Stella, and a peculiarly skinny dog named Ruby. He earned a Bachelor of Arts from Alma College and has been working as a creative artist of some sort for some time.

He spends much of his day with any type of instrument that makes a mark on a page. He enjoys living in the Midwest (and its meteorological uncertainties) and an occasional good time. Craig's impressive artwork can also be seen on the cover of *Year of the Dogman* and *The Haunting of Sigma*, as well as the cover and interior pictures in *The Longquist Adventures: Western Odyssey*.

Stop by and visit Craig's webpage:

http://www.cjtcreative.com

ABOUT THE EDITOR:

Daniel A. Van Beek believes that grammar is an art form. He is the author of one book and has also served as editor on many others, both fiction and nonfiction. Daniel lives with his wife and two young children in Benton Harbor, Michigan.

3203866

Made in the USA